His Favourite Hole

by

Emmy Hoyes

Prologue

Stuart saw the metal pole coming towards him and put his arm up to protect himself. It struck hard and the pain made him want to vomit. Before he could react, another strike. This time on his shoulder. He knew they weren't going to kill him. They just wanted to show him they meant business.

"Rules. You know the rules. You borrow, you pay back," said the large bearded one. He reeked of vodka but didn't seem drunk.

Stuart was on his knees on the muddy tarmac. It was late and the building site was deserted. The foundations for forty executive homes had been poured but he wasn't going to profit from them. Three years ago he had been an overconfident fool, so used to success that he had walked straight into the trap. Cleaning the site of chemicals had ruined him financially and he was still paying for it. He wanted to tell them that if they hadn't kept changing the rules, he would have paid them back a long time ago. Another blow hit the side of his chest, knocking the air out of his lungs.

The two men got into their van and drove off while he remained curled up on the ground. They had spared his face again. They knew he didn't want to tell anyone. He was too proud to admit that he'd made a mistake.

1

Anyone looking inside the beige Nissan Micra would have sworn that the only occupant must have been poured into the driver's seat. Every inch of space was filled with his enormous body. The driver was fifty-four-year-old Graham, who was travelling north on the M6 at fifty mph, forcing lorry after lorry to overtake him. His mind was on the phone call he had received that morning and not on trying to accommodate fellow motorists.

He had not spoken to Melanie for a long time, and he was glad. She had never managed to hide her disapproval of him since they met at his brother Stuart's wedding five years ago. The perfect couple. He, the fit and successful businessman, and she, the gorgeous health-conscious bride. The wedding buffet had been a clean eating haven. Not a grain of salt or sugar as far as the eye could see, just fresh vegetables, super grains, and tofu in a kaleidoscope of colours. It looked amazing, but Melanie had probably thought that his presence next to the buffet had spoilt the effect.

When she had told him about his brother's death she had seemed a bit incoherent and he suspected she wasn't entirely sober.

"Graham? It's me, Melanie."

"Hi, Mela…" Graham started.

"Listen, something awful has happened," Melanie cut in, and Graham could tell she was close to tears. "Stuart's died. I think it's best if you come up as soon as you can."

Graham had needed a few seconds to comprehend what Melanie had just said.

"And bring Dorene," she added.

"Sure," Graham replied.

What followed were some rambling justifications to why this would help Melanie with various arrangements, even though Graham wasn't going to question her requests.

She wrapped up the phone call saying "I don't understand. It's not fair that he's died", with the emphasis just a bit too strongly on "he". In her mind, of the two brothers, Graham should have been the one to die first. He could see her point.

Apparently, his younger brother had died from a heart attack. The news had made Graham's chest tighten up and he could feel his own heart beating faster than normal. If Stuart's heart had decided to pack up, surely he must be living on borrowed time? Nevertheless, he'd be tempted to mention the failure of his brother's virtuous lifestyle to outperform his own sedentary ways when he met Melanie.

Graham had spent a few minutes packing some clothes and a toothbrush into the cheap suitcase that his mum had given him for a school trip at sixteen. He had checked his diary and made a few phone calls to cancel the piano tuning jobs he had scheduled in the days ahead. Business had been pretty slow recently. The advent of good electronic keyboards, or digital pianos as the shop liked to call them, had crippled his business over the last few years. And even he had to admit they were exceptionally good. The other day he had struggled to tell one of the top Roland models from a real piano when visiting the Cloughman and Son's Piano Emporium that generated most of his work. Not only did they take up less space but they were also cheaper than a real piano, especially when taking into account the cost of hiring piano movers and getting the things tuned. He knew he was a dying breed, although he wasn't the one that had died.

2

Graham snapped out of his thoughts just in time to exit the motorway as the signs for Sandbach slipped out of view. Silver Angels Retirement Community had been chosen by Stuart as the new home for their mother Dorene after she had spent a brief period living with him and Melanie. The fact that it was 240 miles from Stuart's home north of Glasgow was a strong indicator that things had not gone well. But he hadn't wanted to pry and had been quite happy to have his mother move closer. It had meant fewer trips up to Scotland and he had only seen his brother once in the last eighteen months, which he now thoroughly regretted.

Graham would regularly go and visit Dorene and it wasn't a bad place, on the contrary. She had started off in the assisted living bungalows, where she had passed most of her time pottering in the communal gardens. Each new resident tending the rose bushes that had life expectancies well above the gardeners themselves. Sadly a couple of "episodes" had forced the home to confiscate her hedging shears and gently persuade her to join the communal lodgings where the less independent clients lived. The official reason was recorded as vascular dementia, to avoid the police getting involved.

The staff were delightful whenever Graham visited,

especially after he had started looking after their precious old Waldstein piano that had been bequeathed to them by one of their residents, a gentleman who had apparently been a famous, exceptionally talented pianist. He didn't have the heart to tell them that their prized piano was just a cheap modern Chinese version and judging by the state it had been in when he first had taken a look at it, it was highly unlikely that the elderly gentleman had been a piano connoisseur.

Graham knew the staff and residents would be disappointed that he hadn't brought his piano tuning tools as he usually did. The first time he looked at the piano it took him a full three hours to get it into shape. While he worked on it, most of the residents had gathered in the lounge, attracted by the unusual sounds. They had watched him for the full duration, in silence, the only interruption being cups of tea handed out by the staff. He realized then how utterly bored they must have been to want to spend most of their afternoon watching a fat guy tune a dilapidated piano. When he finally had stood up and lowered the keyboard cover they had all started applauding. It had touched him to the core and he hadn't known what to do. Seconds later his mother had shuffled up to him with a beaming smile. She had lifted his right arm and they had taken a bow together. From then on he had started to tune the piano each time he visited, a necessity as it went out of tune frustratingly quickly, and then play a few pieces for the residents. From time to time his mother would join him and they would perform duets from his childhood. He was amazed by how well his mother was able to play when often she couldn't remember what she had just had for dinner.

Dorene had changed as she had got older and he would be inclined to say for the better. Like many women who suddenly find themselves without the burden of caring for a husband, children or parents, she had blossomed in her later years. Graham couldn't remember her laughing a lot when he was little, not that she had been a mean mother. Quite the opposite, she had been a very loving parent, just not much fun. When she had finally retired from her headmistress position at Sandbach Church of England School she had got involved in the local amateur dramatics society and Graham had enjoyed helping her rehearse her lines. It was he who had noticed her mental decline before anyone else had. He had gently brought it up a number of times but Dorene had always had an excuse. It was due to the fact she was stressed about finding the right costume or the lack of sleep. There was always an explanation. Her great ability to ad-lib had kept her on the stage for far longer than Graham had expected possible. She had eventually realized that she was letting the rest of the cast down and had retired from the theatre but had continued performing, just not on the stage. She was no longer the serious headmistress, she was Dorene and she didn't mind if people laughed at her for forgetting the punchline to her stupid incoherent jokes, as long as she made people laugh. She was fun now because she didn't care what people thought anymore.

Graham pulled into the visitors' car park and turned

the engine off. A leaf gently floated down from a sycamore tree and settled on the windscreen. He stared at the leaf, buying time before having to meet his mother. He hadn't talked to her directly but had spoken to one of the care assistants about what had happened to Stuart and had asked them to pick a good moment to let Dorene know. He doubted there was such a thing as a good moment to tell a mother about the death of her son.

He slowly eased himself out of the car and walked up the ramp to the main door. He remembered his mother saying that the ramp was there so they could roll out the stretchers with the corpses more easily. He hadn't been sure if it had been a joke or a statement of disapproval of the fact that she had become a resident. Most likely both.

The nurse greeted him with a well-practiced look of sympathy on her face. Yes, she had spoken to Dorene who seemed to have understood what had happened. At least that settled the worst of his fears. The nurse said his mother was waiting for him in her room, bags packed and ready.

"Mum," Graham said after a gentle tap on Dorene's door. "Mum, it's me, can I come in?" He wished he could replicate the gentle look of saintliness that had been present on the nurse's face as he gently opened the door.

"Graham, darling. I'm so sorry, come in." Dorene was slumped in the wingback armchair having, by the looks of it, just woken up. Graham was struck by how small she looked, dressed in a flowery blouse, dark blue polyester trousers, and comfy beige old lady's strolling shoes. She looked tired.

"I'm so sorry mum, I only found out this morning," Graham said while closing the door behind him. "Not sure what to say. Don't think it has sunk in properly. I mean, it was so unexpected." Graham continued.

"Yes," Dorene finally said, "maybe it was." She turned her head to the window facing the internal courtyard, a tranquil but somewhat gloomy place, which boasted a large tree sculpture with hundreds of tiny leaves made of copper. No amateur gardeners required to look after it, but unlike a real tree that varied its appearance depending on the season, this one looked frozen and dead at all times.

Graham looked at the photo in the silver frame proudly displayed on the chest of drawers close to the door. It was of him and Stuart in their mid-teens. His midriff already displaying a robust layer of blubber next to the picture-perfect Stuart, with his bleached hair and tanned slim body. Stuart had one arm around Graham and the other around his new surfboard. Even at twelve, he was already more confident than his older brother, as they stood in front of large barnacle-covered rocks on a Cornish beach smiling to the camera.

"Shall we go?" Graham suggested, conscious of the 240-mile drive ahead of them. He picked up Dorene's suitcase.

Without replying, his mother slowly got out of the chair. He tried not to notice the dark wet patch left on the seat as they both left the room.

3

Doreen was very quiet in the car. Graham couldn't see her face, as she was facing away from him and had started to worry she might have passed away or perhaps had sunk into a very bad mood. He pulled off at Tebay services and was relieved to discover that she had merely been asleep. He had often stopped at this service station on the way up to see Stuart. Not only was the food good, but there was a well-stocked farm shop to pick up some gifts to avoid arriving empty-handed.

He woke Dorene up and walked her to the restrooms as a precaution. Graham waited outside the ladies and couldn't help thinking how the roles had reversed. He had just started to worry about having to go in and find her when she appeared, with a long piece of toilet paper trailing behind her that was stuck to the heel of her shoe. They went into the farm shop section and Graham reluctantly walked past the meat counter. He had often bought some nice steaks or a large Cumberland sausage, but Stuart had gone vegetarian since he met Melanie. He was contemplating whether to buy an overpriced piece of smoked tofu when Dorene joined him holding a colourful wooden jigsaw of farm animals.

"I'm going to get this for Tom," she announced. Graham was about to speak and then waited for a couple of seconds while looking at Dorene. Dorene started to sense that something was wrong.

"Mum, Tom is eighteen," he finally said.

"I knew that. I'll see if I can find something else." She went back to the gift section.

In the end, Graham bought a bottle of organic white wine, a box of giant couscous made by a women's cooperative in Palestine, and some local Cumbrian ewe's cheese. He wasn't sure it was vegetarian, but if nobody else wanted it, he'd happily eat it all himself. Dorene had returned with a large bag of Haribo sweets for Tom. They returned to the car and continued the journey north.

He had never been to Stuart's house before, as he and Melanie had bought it only six months earlier. The house was called Eagle's Nest Manor. Why not just call it Eyrie Manor? Graham thought to himself, amused.

He was slightly worried he might have the wrong postcode, as the satnav showed he was less than a minute away and he was still was weaving through post-war housing estates. At least the golf course was also signposted in the same direction, which offered him some comfort. Stuart would never live any further than walking distance from a golf course. Graham had joined Stuart a couple of times for a round and to his surprise had enjoyed it. It was probably the only sport he felt he could take part in without attracting ridicule. He had thought of joining a local golf club, but without Stuart's presence to boost his confidence, he had failed to muster enough courage to apply for membership.

He drove past the golf course gates and a couple of

hundred metres later the satnav made a cheerful ping and the polite computerised female voice announced that they had reached their destination. He was in front of a wide, paved drive with an oversized carved stone sign saying Kilmardinny Gardens. It had been symmetrically planted with cordylines and grasses typical for modern executive housing developments. He cautiously drove through the gates into the estate, surprised that the mansion his brother had bought was perhaps not as manor-like as he had been led to believe.

As he slowly worked his way around the crescent he realised that the houses, despite being on an estate, were by no means cheap. They were large and ostentatious but packed close together, which made them look like toy versions of proper manors and mansions. The developers had designed them all slightly different, but not so different that you would be able to remember any one of them in particular. Graham slowly drove along the street, trying to read one brass plaque after another. "Albatross Court", "High Green Ways" and "Birdie mansion". Nice theme. He finally found "Eagle's Nest Manor" and pulled into the large driveway that widened out sufficiently to have a circular raised bed in the middle of it containing a slightly underwhelming monkey puzzle tree.

Dorene woke up as he turned off the engine. Graham quickly extracted himself from the driver's seat and went over and opened the passenger door to help his mother out of the car. If he was lucky, he might still have a dry passenger seat. Once Dorene was out, they walked together to the front entrance and he rang the doorbell twice in quick succession.

"Come in, both of you!" Melanie exclaimed as she opened the heavily varnished door. Both of us, well that's nice Graham thought, wondering if she perhaps thought that one of them might have preferred to remain outside. Melanie quickly ushered Dorene to the hallway toilet and pretty much pushed her in and closed the door. Graham couldn't help admire the swiftness of her actions and realised that, of course, they had had some practice when Dorene had been living with them. He looked at Melanie's face and despite his intense dislike of her, he couldn't help feeling sorry for her. Even though her billowy red hair looked as good as it always did, her face was puffy, like after a night of heavy drinking. Her eyes were swollen and red, which ironically set her green irises off beautifully. Graham had never seen Melanie in any other state than perfect, so being confronted by a real person threw him off his guard.

"You ok?" he let slip before cursing himself for asking such a stupid thing.

"Not really," Melanie replied before looking straight up at the ceiling to try and prevent her eyes from spilling tears down her face.

The last four words of conversation were probably the most honest and intimate he and Melanie had ever had and he was suddenly overcome with sympathy for her. He took a step forward and embraced her very spindly figure to comfort her. A split second later he felt her stiffen up and arch her back awkwardly to avoid his belly touching her and the moment was gone. He quickly lifted his arms off her shoulders and took a step back. She hadn't changed, she was still Melanie after all. Not wasting a moment to make sure he knew she disapproved of him.

"How are you?" she asked him, putting on a neutral and business-like face. She didn't wait for him to reply before she started walking towards the kitchen muttering "Would you like a cup of tea?" It didn't seem like she needed an answer to that question either so Graham silently followed her.

Melanie was Stuart's third wife. Graham could only guess that she had got her way when it came to the interior design of this house as it didn't look anything like the other houses that Stuart had lived in. It was very modern and minimalist. Cream tiled floors, white walls with accent pieces that seem to serve no purpose other than to look expensive. When he entered the living room area he was both surprised and delighted to see Dorene's upright Steinway piano. It was a beautiful piece, built in Germany around 1890 and veneered in burr walnut. Far too ornate for Melanie, Graham thought and probably one of the few items left from when Dorene had lived with them. He knew the instrument inside out as it was the piano he learnt to play on. It irritated him that Stuart had it because as far as he knew, Stuart had never learnt to play.

"Sugar?" came Melanie's matter-of-fact voice from the kitchen area. She had clearly managed to compose herself again.

"Just the one please," Graham replied. He suddenly felt the full realisation of what had happened. Stuart was gone. And he missed him. Stuart would have offered him a cold beer and they would have sat down in front of the TV, chatting away or being quiet, didn't matter. Despite being so different, they had been very close.

"What happened?" he asked as Melanie handed him his cup of tea.

She turned her face towards the patio doors and gave a slight nod. "Apparently, he had a heart attack in the garden." She looked uncomfortable and Graham thought it suited her. "I was out that night and when I got back the ambulance had been and gone".

They were interrupted by Tom bursting into the kitchen area, looking taller and thinner than Graham thought physically possible. Tom was Stuart's son by Susie, his second wife.

"Who the hell is locked in the downstairs loo?"

4

"You need to turn the lock, Dorene." Melanie said in a louder and more patronising way than the situation required.

"I HAVE turned the lock and it doesn't open." Dorene's irritated voice came back.

"Yes, you have locked it because it wasn't locked in the first place!" Melanie replied.

"I might have a slight problem with my memory but I still know how a bathroom door works. I tried lots of times and it won't open!" A few metallic rattles followed proving that something wasn't quite right with the locking mechanism.

Melanie looked up at Graham and Tom, in a way that told them she expected them to take over from here. Which made Tom look at Graham with a quirky smile on his face.

"I bet you wouldn't need much of a run-up to break down the door? I mean…."

Before Tom continued, Graham stopped him and said "I think we'll probably just get a screwdriver".

While Melanie went off to search for a screwdriver, Tom and Graham exchanged condolences, both knowing that at some point they had to acknowledge to each other what had happened.

"Is this where you live now?" Graham asked.

"Not really, just the odd night every now and again when Mum gets on my nerves," Tom replied just as Melanie came back with a box containing various tools.

"He's been a star! For two days now he's been here helping me sort stuff out. You've gone through every room, cleaning and tidying, haven't you Tom?

Graham noticed Tom looked a little uncomfortable. Tom cleaning? Graham knew what Tom's bedroom usually looked like and tidying certainly wasn't his strong side. Perhaps he had a crush on Melanie?

Later that night, after successfully releasing Dorene from captivity, they all gathered around the dining room table over delivery pizzas. The atmosphere was relaxed with everyone helping themselves to slices straight from the cardboard boxes. There wasn't much conversation as everyone was focusing on eating their fair share of pizza.

"So, what are the plans?" Graham asked Melanie when the last slice of pizza had gone. He was pleased that he hadn't eaten more even if he could easily have managed at least double that amount.

"Sorry, I should have told you when you arrived. It's become complicated. The coroner phoned this lunchtime and they're still waiting for the autopsy. And I was hoping we could have the funeral on Friday…. well, that doesn't look likely now." Melanie said with a sigh and continued by describing the arrangements she had already made with the undertaker. Dorene got involved and the two of them started discussing the flowers. Tom was glued to his phone.

Graham felt confused. How did Melanie know that

he had died from a heart attack if the autopsy results weren't available yet? What had Stuart been doing in the garden late at night?

"Hey Graham, fancy a dip in the hot tub?" Tom suddenly asked, causing Graham to nearly jump out of his skin. Before Graham managed to process the question and mentally confirm that he didn't even own a set of swimming trunks, never mind having brought them with him, Melanie replied "Sorry Tom, the hot tub is a no-go area at the moment."

"Why? It was fine a few days ago, what's up with it? Tom asked like he thought Melanie was making it up to prevent him from having fun.

"It's where your Dad... where he... you know... where they found him." Melanie was struggling to find the right words.

"Yeah, but that doesn't mean it's broken does it?" Tom replied in a way that made Graham think it wasn't always easy to have a teenager living with you.

"So Melanie, was he electrocuted, or did he shit in it?" Dorene suddenly piped up and then added "Or both?" leaving the rest of them speechless.

All eyes were now on Melanie.

"The latter," she finally admitted. "I've got a man coming at the weekend to deal with it."

While everyone was clearing the table from empty pizza boxes and plates, a slight figure in the semi-darkness silently scaled the back fence in the garden and approached the little gazebo containing the hot tub.

5

The next morning Graham woke up and for a moment couldn't remember where he was. He had forgotten to pack his sleep apnoea machine, but as far as he could tell, he didn't feel too bad. He'd manage a few days without it. He flung his leg over the side of the bed and sat up looking down on the floor which was covered with scatter cushions. He was reluctant to put them back on the bed as no matter how hard he tried they would always end up looking like a pile of dirty laundry and it felt like such a waste of time.

Graham walked downstairs and found Melanie in the kitchen scrolling through her Facebook feed and greeted her good morning.

"Your mum asked me where Stuart is," Melanie said without looking up from her phone. "I told her to look in the garden. I can't be breaking the news to her over and over again. You go and tell her."

Graham went out through the patio doors and wandered down the recently mowed lawn. He couldn't see Melanie doing much gardening, not with those nails, so they must have a gardener. It took him a while to locate Dorene as she was standing in a hidden corner by the compost heap, looking at a lone sunflower that had taken up residence in amongst the soggy grass clippings.

"Graham, you know.... a garden without weeds is like a life without surprises." Dorene had a thing about weeds. She thought they should be left alone if they had rewarded us with pretty flowers without asking for anything in return. Not ruthlessly pulled out. Numerous times it had caused controversy with her fellow residents at the retirement home and in the end resulting in an energetic attack on a gentleman pulling out some flowering purple loosestrife. She kept looking at the flower while Graham was trying to think of how to tell her about Stuart.

Just as he was about to speak, she said "I remember now. I admit I'd forgotten when I got up this morning. But then I saw the hot tub and it came back to me."

Graham and Dorene walked back to the house and had breakfast with Melanie on the freshly oiled decking outside the kitchen. It was late September and this was probably the last time this year they would be able to eat outside.

Melanie had just finished pouring everyone's coffees when a woman's face surrounded by bleached, neatly styled hair popped up over the fence. She called "Good morning!" in a way that was meant to sound spontaneous but clearly wasn't. The woman reminded Graham of one of his regular clients. She looked like the kind of person that thought a piano was a beautiful piece of furniture rather than a musical instrument.

"I'm so sorry about what happened," she continued. Melanie got up and walked towards her. "Did she tell you? I was the one who phoned the ambulance," the woman continued now addressing Graham and Dorene.

"Terrible thing. If it hadn't been for that young girl he might have been there all night. Such a shame he didn't make it. He was such a lovely…" At this point, Melanie had reached the fence and interrupted her. She was speaking quietly so the others couldn't hear what she was saying.

"Would you like to come over for a cup of coffee?" Dorene suddenly called out. Graham admired his mum's ability to think so quickly despite her deteriorating mind.

"Please do, we have plenty," Graham added to make up for Melanie's less than impressed facial expression.

"Oh, that would be lovely. I'll just nip out the front and come over. Neighbours have to support each other in difficult times, don't they?" And just as quickly as the head had appeared, it was gone again. Thirty seconds later she joined them on the decking.

"Hi, I'm Helen," she announced, waving to Graham and Dorene, as neither of them had made an attempt to get up. Dorene had taken advantage of being old, and gave a cheerful wave back and said "I'm Dorene, Stuart's mother, and this is Graham, my other son." She nodded towards Graham. He was concerned that the patio chair might not release its grip on him as its armrests were hugging his waist in a worrying way. Helen seemed satisfied with them waving politely and carried on. "I can't describe how awful I felt, being home alone when it happened. And that shriek! I mean it was a good thing. It certainly got me out of bed and looking out of the window. That's when I saw that gorgeous young girl standing there totally beside herself."

With every word, Melanie's face was turning a shade darker. "Do you take sugar?" she interrupted. Helen, who had faced Graham and Dorene up until then, suddenly turned her head and looked straight at Melanie. "Did you know he came over in the afternoon and asked me and Mike to witness his will?"

Melanie's face went from dark purple to ghostly white in the matter of a second as she failed to stop pouring the coffee in Helen's cup, letting it overflow. "Oh gosh, I'll get a cloth," she muttered while escaping back into the kitchen.

There was an awkward silence. Graham was desperate to know more but wasn't sure about what to ask. He felt Melanie hadn't told him the full truth about what had happened and hoped Dorene might take the lead.

"Do you live nearby?" Dorene gently enquired of Helen, like the last five minutes never had taken place.

Helen seemed confused and looked at Graham for some kind of explanation.

"Yes Mum, she is the neighbour," Graham said in a way that made it clear to Helen that this was Dorene's problem, not hers.

Melanie returned with several sheets of kitchen roll. "Let me mop this up," she said in a strained voice as she leaned over the table giving the appearance of having collected herself.

"Dolce & Gabbana isn't it?" Helen said.

"What do you mean?" Melanie replied.

"Your perfume," Helen said in a way that indicated

that the fight was still on. Without waiting for a response, she turned to Graham and Dorene and said how nice it had been to meet them and that she would leave them to their breakfast and left as suddenly as she had appeared.

Graham was still trying to process everything that Helen had said. He couldn't help taking pleasure in Helen's stunt even though it had seemed unnecessarily cruel considering the recent tragedy.

6

Tom still felt tired when he woke up. His phone was out of charge but he could tell it was late as the sun was high in the sky. He had done more tidying and cleaning in the last two days than previously in his entire life. It wasn't the actual cleaning that had tired him out. It was the horrible feeling in his stomach that had reinserted itself within seconds of waking up. It was bad enough that Dad was dead, but to think he might have been the one that had killed him made it almost unbearable. If only he could find the clear little plastic bag he had given his dad on Friday night, the last time he had seen him alive. If it still contained the white grainy powder perhaps he might not be the one to blame.

Six months ago he had thought it quite cool that his dad had asked if he could get him some weed. At first, Tom had thought it was a trick question. If he said yes, he might be in for a very long and serious lecture about the dangers of drugs. But his dad had immediately asked him not to tell his mum or Melanie, so Tom had answered truthfully, that yes, of course he could get hold of some weed. It had worked out as a nice little earner and had ended up paying for Tom's own modest use.

After dinner on Friday, his dad had suggested they play a game of pool in the games' room, which was the cue for swapping a £20 note for a small bag of marijuana. This time Tom had also handed him a small sachet of KET. His friend Jack had given him a free sample and it only seemed fair to share. Or so he justified it, when in fact he was a bit worried about trying something different. At least weed was herbal, so it couldn't be that bad for you could it? His plan was to see if his dad wanted to try it and then make the decision whether to try it himself. Stuart had not been impressed when he was given the little plastic bag. Instead, he had given Tom a stern telling off and had asked him to never accept anything or buy anything ever again from this friend of his. He had finished the lecture by saying: "Over my dead body should my son get into serious drugs." And now his dad was dead. To make matters worse the bag, if found, would have his fingerprints on it.

He felt under the pillow and found the other phone. The phone that wasn't his. He had found it on Sunday morning when searching around the hot tub. It had been wedged between the slats of the wooden decking and it had taken him ages to fish it out. He was certain it wasn't Melanie's or his dad's as it had a very tacky glittery pink phone cover. The lock screen had a photo of two sets of bare legs in a hammock with a very nice lush garden in the background. It looked vaguely familiar, but then again, Instagram was flooded with people's pictures of their own legs and feet.

When he found it, it had eight missed calls from someone called Anna. He didn't know an Anna and since the phone was locked he couldn't phone this Anna back to find out who the owner of the phone was. He just had to wait until the phone rang again so he could answer it. He had carried it around for a bit but felt that now was not the time to look like a drug dealer with pockets full of mobiles and had decided to leave it under the pillow.

It had no new messages or missed calls.

He stood up and immediately tripped over his trainers that were discarded by the side of the bed. He found his crumpled-up t-shirt and put it on. It didn't smell too good. He really needed to go back home to get some clean clothes. Perhaps Graham could give him a lift. He really liked Uncle Graham, and so did his mum. Yes, that would be a good plan. He could then get a lift straight back again and continue his search as he still had the garage and garden shed to go through.

He put on the rest of his clothes and walked downstairs just in time to see a blond woman he'd never seen before leave the house. His immediate thought was that perhaps she had come to look for her phone. There was no way that the photo on the lock screen was of her legs, so Tom decided not to risk it and said nothing.

He grabbed a banana in the kitchen and continued out to the deck where he found the others in silence. From the look on their faces, something traumatic had clearly taken place. It reminded him of what it was like before his mum and dad had split up. For a period they had decided not to speak to each other and instead use him as a go-between. It was like they were both waiting for the other to finally say that it was over, as neither were prepared to move out. Graham had visited a couple of times during this period and his parents had suddenly behaved as if everything was fine. Tom had never understood how they could suddenly switch to being reasonable and polite, even laughing together, as soon as they had a visitor. If they were able to do that then why couldn't they do it when nobody was watching?

As an only child, Tom had been used to fighting for attention from adults, but Graham had given it to him unprompted and never let his phone compete for his attention. Graham had always talked to Tom as a person and not just a child and had always said yes to playing board games, something his parents had given up on a long time ago.

Tom noticed that Melanie was staring towards the bottom of the garden while Dorene was for some reason folding wet and coffee-stained pieces of kitchen roll into neat bundles. Not knowing what else to say, he looked at Graham and said "My mum would like to see you. Any chance you could give me a lift home and I could get some clean clothes?"

"Sure, we can go now if you want?" Graham replied, "You don't mind, do you?" he then asked Melanie and Dorene as he made sure he pushed down firmly on the armrests of the patio chair as he stood up.

"Sure, of course not," Melanie replied.

They left the house before anyone changed their mind. Tom felt grateful that he now had Graham to himself. He had been thinking during the night that Graham might be the only person he could tell about his worries. He opened the door to the Micra and sat down in the passenger seat and felt something cold and wet soaking into his jeans. "Whoa… what's that!?" he cried out and immediately got up again.

"Sorry, that will be Grandma, you'd better sit in the back," Graham replied with a sigh. Tom flipped the seat forward and got in the back.

They headed out of the estate and Tom gave Graham directions to Scotstoun which was less than quarter of an hour away. Graham had been to Susie's place before but wasn't familiar with the route from Stuart's new place.

"Any chance we could stop off at McDonald's?" Tom asked tentatively. "I mean, only if you want to," he added, like he was preparing himself for a rejection.

"Sure, why not," Graham replied and followed Tom's directions. In less than a minute they were pulling into the car park. Graham had to admit he was starving. Melanie seemed to think coffee and a glass of orange juice constituted breakfast and probably would have given him one of her disapproving looks had he asked for something more substantial.

"Here's £20, get what you want and get a bacon and egg McMuffin for me," Graham said, handing the note across his shoulder. Tom didn't take it though, which left his arm hovering awkwardly in the air.

"Can you go? I look like I've wet my pants," Tom said rather timidly, "and smell like it too."

"OK, fair enough," Graham replied. He went inside and joined the queue. He wasn't a regular MacDonald's customer and was quite surprised how busy the place was. When it was his turn he ordered his McMuffin and a double sausage and egg one with a hash brown for Tom as requested. He cursed himself for not using the drive-thru. At least with two people in the car, the order wouldn't have seemed so gluttonous and he started to feel self-conscious. He quickly calmed down when he realized that he wasn't the largest person in the queue. Not even the second largest. It was a weirdly comforting feeling that he had rarely felt before.

He had always had a large frame but the actual weight hadn't started to pile on until just before puberty. His dad had died suddenly when Graham was twelve and his mother had struggled to cope. She had become depressed, although of course he hadn't known that, as children in those days weren't well versed in psychiatry. He had realized that he could temporarily make her happy by ensuring the plates were empty after every meal; a role that his dad, a large and hungry man, had performed very well up until his death. She was used to cooking large amounts of food and found it difficult to adjust to there being only the three of them at the table. Graham kept eating as he only wanted his mum to be happy again. By the time she recovered from her depression, just over a year later, he had turned into a rather tubby child. Stuart had not put any weight on as he had always been a picky eater. Despite her efforts to introduce healthy foods Graham had already got used to eating more than he required, a habit he had retained for the whole of his life. Instead, she had placed her focus on making Stuart stay slim and healthy while Graham had often wondered why she hadn't been stricter with him as well.

Stuart had been a very fidgety child and had struggled to sit still, especially at school. He soon was channelling his extra energy into sport and gained a place on both the rugby and the cricket teams. With sporting success came confidence and popularity, something Graham had never managed to obtain. Graham had tried to impress with his dedication to his schoolwork while Stuart had done the minimum to get the teachers off his back, and often paid Graham to complete his homework for him. It had felt slightly unfair in Graham's mind that by the time they both were in their twenties Stuart was already earning twice as much and was driving around in a brand new Audi selling gym equipment to the booming fitness industry.

Tom and Graham decided to eat in the car. Tom was quiet and Graham could tell there was something on his mind. It was hardly surprising though, he had just lost his dad. They finished their breakfast and drove the remaining five minutes to Susie's house.

7

Helen opened her kitchen window to see if she could hear what was being said on next-door's patio. She wasn't confident enough to go outside as Melanie might have gathered herself enough to retaliate over the fence. Despite getting as close to the window as she dared, she couldn't hear anything or even see if anyone was still out there. Not like last Saturday lunchtime when she and Mike could hear Stuart and Melanie having a massive quarrel in the garden. It was a shame as she would have loved to gauge the effects of what she had said. She knew falling out with neighbours rarely ended well but she hadn't been able to resist the opportunity to confront Melanie.

Helen didn't mind Stuart. He was always polite, even if purely in a superficial way. It was Melanie she couldn't stand, especially since Mike seemed to really like her. She had caught the two of them chatting over the garden fence a few times and she could tell by the way Melanie smiled and giggled that she was trying to seduce Mike. Or so it seemed anyway. When she joined the conversation it had immediately become much less jovial and she had a distinct feeling that they had not wanted her company. She couldn't be sure though. She had accused Mike many times of being unfaithful, especially in the early years of their marriage. As a junior doctor Mike had had to spend many nights on-call at the hospital while Helen had fretted at home alone full of self-doubt. All the accusations had turned out to be false and she had ended up feeling even worse than before. She hadn't confronted him with her worries or suspicions for a while now as she couldn't afford to be wrong again. She didn't want to come across as an insecure and jealous wife, although that is exactly what she was. She was desperate to hide it, as there is nothing more unattractive than jealousy.

She had been very surprised on Saturday afternoon when Stuart had knocked on the door holding a brown envelope. She had invited him in and gone to get Mike from the bottom of the garden where he had been digging up this year's crop of Désirée potatoes. Stuart had seemed subdued when he asked them to be the witnesses of his new will. They had sat down at the kitchen table and Helen had spent an awkwardly long time looking through cupboards and drawers trying to find a working pen. Stuart had extracted two sheets of A4 from the envelope, quickly turning the first page upside down. He signed at the bottom of the second sheet and turned the sheet around for Helen and Mike to put their names down as witnesses. She didn't have much time to read any of the content, but she couldn't help thinking that this had something to do with the big argument she had overheard earlier that day.

Afterwards, she had wanted to chat with Mike about what had made Stuart want to change his will, but Mike hadn't seemed at all intrigued and had dismissed her by telling her she shouldn't be so nosey. As usual, she had extrapolated this to mean far more than had actually been said. He had gone back to his digging after causally having reminded her that he was on call again this evening. She had felt a large lump developing in her throat and a vague feeling of nausea. She hadn't wanted to ask him why, all of a sudden, he seemed to be on call so much, as she knew he'd just say that there were staffing issues at the Queen Elizabeth hospital.

Later that evening she had consulted Google Maps to find out how far the hospital was from their home so she could start checking his car's mileage to see if she could either get some reassurance or some evidence of him lying. She hadn't expected that she would be driving there herself so soon thereafter.

Helen went up to her bedroom to get a better view of Melanie's patio. She now felt trapped in her own house and the triumphant feeling she had had earlier while deliberately trying to unsettle Melanie was now replaced by anxiety having recalled Saturday's events.

She opened the curtains and the patio was now empty and the coffee cups had been taken inside. She glanced towards the gazebo and the image from Saturday night of the naked young girl screaming was still vivid in her mind. She remembered having taken a Temazepam to help her get to sleep but had been dragged up to the surface of consciousness by a high pitched cry of terror. She had remained frozen at the window, letting her brain get back up to speed, before she had grabbed a dressing gown and headed out onto the street at the front. She had rung the doorbell but nobody had answered. The front door had been unlocked so she had walked in, calling out "Hello" as she had worked her way to the back of the house. She remembered that there had been a couple of empty champagne bottles on the kitchen table and the patio doors had been open. There had been no sign of the girl in the garden. For a moment she had stood there wondering if it had all just been a bad dream.

She then had heard the whirl of the hot tub jets. That, and the blue glow had made her walk towards the gazebo. At first she hadn't seen anything out of the ordinary, but as she had got closer she had seen Stuart's face just above the surface of the water. Mouth open, eyes open, like he had seen a ghost. He was suspended in a pool of darkish water. Her first thought had been that he must have tried to commit suicide, as that somehow tied in with having changed his will only hours earlier. But both wrists had been intact. She had fished her phone out of her dressing gown pocket and called for an ambulance. The call handler had wanted her to check his breathing and start administering CPR but she had been reluctant. She had known he was dead. She had worked as a nursing assistant when she had met Mike and had seen enough dead people to easily recognize one.

Just after the ambulance had left, Melanie had pulled up in a taxi. She had looked very surprised and a tad bit suspicious seeing Helen, wearing a dressing gown, outside her own house. Helen hadn't wasted any time before telling Melanie about what had happened. She had even offered to drive Melanie to the hospital as a way of avoiding having to pass on the most important piece of information regarding the state of Stuart's health. She had felt very ambivalent as they travelled in silence to the hospital. She wasn't sure if she felt sorry for Melanie or not. She ought to of course, but the dislike of her neighbour was running deep enough for her to almost feel slightly pleased about Melanie's loss. With any luck, she would be forced to move.

She had dropped off Melanie by the entrance to A&E and had offered to wait for her. An idiotic suggestion, no doubt made to compensate for the horrid thoughts she had had during the journey. Thankfully her offer had been declined and she had returned home. Only too late had she realised she should have swung by the staff car park to see if she could have spotted Mike's car. There would have been no harm in checking.

When she got home she had gone straight back to bed after taking a second Temazepam, only to wake up briefly when Mike got into the bed beside her. She had noticed the sweet scent of vanilla on his face as he had leant over to give her a kiss but the tablet had battered her suspicious mind enough to let her drift off immediately afterwards.

As Helen stood in her bedroom, still looking out over next door's garden a thought suddenly hit her. Now Stuart was dead, only she stood in the way of Mike and Melanie's   happy   future   together.

8

When Graham and Tom arrived back at Eagle's Nest Manor late in the afternoon there was a police car on the drive. It was parked in such a way that Graham would be forced to block it in, so instead he chose to reverse out and leave his car on the street. Had he used the rearview mirror, instead of his side mirrors, he would have spotted Tom looking whiter than a sheet.

Two uniformed female police officers were crowding the hallway as Graham and Tom came through the door. The taller of the two was speaking into a radio handset. "Yes, I think we'll need the search dogs. Could you call them out for me? Also, we could do with a couple of extra officers searching the house and garden." Tom tried to hide his mounting panic, but started to feel faint. His saliva glands were going into overdrive and his ears started humming. Before anyone had time to address him, he was throwing up in the downstairs loo.

"You ok?" Graham asked, when Tom returned to the hallway a few minutes later, thankful that the police officers had gone to a different room.

"Must be something I ate," Tom replied while avoiding making eye contact. "What's the police doing here? he asked tentatively.

"Grandma has gone missing," Graham replied.

"They want to ask us some questions after they have finished talking to Melanie." Tom turned to Graham with a quizzical look. "Grandma missing? But they said they needed to search the house? Do they think we mislaid her or something?"

"I don't know, I guess we'll know more soon," Graham replied and sat down on the stairs.

A few minutes later one of the officers came back and summoned them to join Melanie in the kitchen.

"Melanie says you and Dorene arrived yesterday. And neither of you have been here before. Is that correct?" the shorter and stockier officer asked Graham.

"Yes, that's right," Graham replied.

"Can you think of any reason why she would've left the house on her own?" came the follow-up question.

"No, not really. When Tom and I left she was here and was absolutely fine. We've just come back and don't really know what's happened." Graham looked at Melanie hoping she could fill in the missing pieces.

While a crackly message came through on the radio, Tom leaned forward quietly saying to Graham "Is this because she is demented?"

"Actually we prefer to call them vulnerable when we're referring to a missing person with dementia or Alzheimer's," the stocky officer interrupted before Graham had thought of an answer. "We will get as many resources on this as we can," she continued as she folded her notebook and stood up. "It's not likely she's gone far at this point. We tend to find three quarters of vulnerable people within a couple of miles of where they were last seen. We'll start by searching the house and back garden. No offence, but you'd be surprised how often we find people much closer than you'd expect."

The doorbell rang and Tom got up and let another two officers into the house. The radios were going off all the time and it was a miracle that anyone could tell what was being said. Tom certainly couldn't.

"Do you need to look in my room?" he asked the young Asian officer he had just let in. "Just that I feel a bit tired and think I need to go for a nap. I've got food poisoning."

"Sure, I'll come with you and take a look straight away," the officer said and together they walked up the stairs.

While the house and garden were being searched thoroughly, Graham asked Melanie if there was something he should know about all this.

"No, one minute she was here and the next she was gone! Obviously, I've looked all over the house already. Not sure why the police have to look again. I'd know if she was here or not!" she replied in a sarcastic fashion.

"I suppose they can't just rule out foul play," Graham added.

"Surely you don't think I've got anything to do with it!" Melanie exclaimed.

"Of course not," Graham replied, "they'll just be following protocol."

After half an hour the four officers gathered back in the kitchen. They hadn't found anything and told Graham and Melanie that they were going to set up a base at the golf course clubhouse from where they could coordinate the search. They would be in touch as soon as they had any news and it would be great if Graham or Melanie could pop down with a photo of Dorene as soon as possible.

Once the team had left, the house became unnaturally quiet. Melanie got a box of photos out of the dining room sideboard and sat down at the table. Graham joined her and together they looked at the various photos that the box contained. Some of them were at least 20 years old, if not even older. Plenty were of Tom as a baby and some of Stuart's previous wives. There was even the odd one that Graham was in.

"You haven't got any more recent ones than these?" Graham asked.

"I'm afraid not. The only other photos I have are on my phone, but I haven't exactly been busy taking photos of your Mum with it, have I?" Melanie replied defensively. "I'm sure Stuart would have some on his phone but it's out of charge and I don't know his password anyway." Melanie continued.

Graham picked up a photo of Stuart posing with his red chopper bike with Graham standing awkwardly in the background holding a traditional racer. His dad had bought the racer and hardly used it and eventually Graham had grown into it. He neither loved nor hated it, it was a means of getting to places. Stuart on the other hand had saved up for his chopper and was hardly seen off it. He would suggest cycling to places just to go out on it and Graham had reluctantly gone with him to keep his mum happy. She was worried that Stuart might get into trouble on his own. The only time Graham had seen trouble was when a gang of boys his own age had shouted "Here comes Laurel and Hardy!" He would have just cycled past the group, ignoring them, but to his horror Stuart had stopped and got off his bike. He had quickly identified the leader, who had tried to impress his friends with his witty remark. Without wasting a second he had walked up to him and had punched his nose so hard that the spotty teen had fallen over. His friends had just stood there as if they had been frozen, too scared to even say anything. Stuart had got back on his bike and they had cycled off together. Neither of them had ever mentioned what had happened to anyone, and Graham had realised that it was Stuart looking out for him, rather than the other way around.

"Here is one we could use," Melanie suddenly announced and held up a photo of Dorene with Tom on her lap. Tom was probably about five years old but despite the photo being old, Dorene was easily recognizable. She was wearing a shiny blue cone-shaped party hat on her head, but it would have to do. Dorene had now been missing for four hours.

"Walk or drive?" Melanie asked.

"We could walk I suppose," Graham replied.

They put their coats on as the sun was now low in the sky and the nice warmth from this morning was long gone. It had started to drizzle by the time they got to the clubhouse. Two police cars, a police transit van, and a dog unit were parked in the golf course car park and a mountain rescue Landrover turned up just as Graham and Melanie arrived at the main entrance. They followed the stream of uniformed personnel to the main event room past the bar area. A large television screen on a stand had been set up displaying an aerial photo with a bright green circle drawn using the computer with the Kilmardinny Gardens estate in its centre. A large whiteboard was placed next to the screen and had Dorene's description on it, 79 years, 154 cm, grey hair, slight build, light blue jacket and dark trousers. Melanie's address was also on it and a group of police officers were gathered in front of the board being briefed. Areas on the map were being sectioned off with more green and pink lines and every minute or so a small team would break off and presumably go to their designated search area. While Graham and Melanie were waiting, the group was joined by more people wearing bright red mountain rescue jackets.

After a few minutes the young Asian officer came up to greet them and Melanie handed the photo of Dorene over.

"Thanks, that's brilliant. We'll scan it in and send it out straight away." He took a look at the photo and smiled. "We'll find her, don't worry."

"If you want to wait in the bar, I'll give the photo back to you in a few minutes," the young man said and turned to one of his colleagues to show him the photo.

Before they managed to leave the room, a round-faced ginger-haired policewoman came up and also reassured them that everything possible was being done. "Most often we find them just wandering about on the road you know."

"And if they aren't wandering around on the road, where are they then?" Graham asked.

"Well, that depends. Dementia makes people do the weirdest things. They don't quite reason the way we do. Sometimes they will just carry on in a straight line, even at a junction. They won't turn and instead just keep going even if it means crawling through a hedge. We've found a few under bushes or stuck in brambles you know. I'm sure it won't take long before she is home and safe." The radio went off and the officer rejoined the group in front of the board, while Graham and Melanie went to the bar.

Graham offered to buy Melanie a drink, which she gratefully accepted. Graham had nearly finished his pint of Tennent's lager before the officer came back with the photo.

"Sorry for the delay," he said as he handed over the photo of Dorene. "We'll let you know as soon as we find her."

Graham paid the pretty blond girl working behind the bar for the drinks. She looked unsettled, as if she couldn't make her mind up whether to say something as she gave him his change. She must have decided not to because she turned around and started stocking the fridge with mixers.

It was raining more heavily as they walked home in silence.

Back at the house, there was a note on the kitchen table left by Tom, saying he had gone back to his Mum's house and for them to call him if there was any news about Dorene.

"I suppose all we can do now is wait," Melanie muttered.

"I'm sure we'll hear something soon with so many people searching," Graham replied, as Melanie was pouring gin into a tumbler. "Want one?" she asked, holding up a bottle of a small batch Scottish gin.

"Yes, please," Graham replied. Melanie got another glass out and poured a very healthy triple measure.

"Tonic? Only got slim-line." She looked up apologetically at Graham.

"Sure, slim-line's fine," he replied and chuckled, "I'm sure I'll cope." Melanie's facial expression softened and gave way to a genuine laugh and a smile that was truly addictive. Graham could suddenly see why Stuart had fallen in love with Melanie. The alcohol consumed on empty stomachs had made them put their guards down and the tension present during the last couple of days had gone.

"Right, I'll start on dinner," Melanie said and finished her gin and tonic in one sweep.

"Anything you don't eat?" She asked while looking into the large American-style fridge freezer.

Dinner had consisted of halloumi and roasted pepper wraps with three kinds of hummus that Melanie apologised for not having made herself. Graham wasn't too fussed about vegetarian food but found the meal surprisingly pleasant. It helped that they had shared a bottle of Rioja while eating it.

They left the dishes in the kitchen and made

45

themselves comfortable on the sofas in the living room. Melanie switched the TV on, but even though both of them gazed at the screen, neither of them was actually watching. Melanie got up and started pacing. She sat down again and changed channels, but within five minutes she stood up and walked over to the window facing the street. The alcohol had started to wear off and had been replaced by anxiety. It was now ten o'clock and it was dark outside and still raining.

"How come you seem so calm?" Melanie asked Graham, still looking out of the window even though she could mainly see her own reflection.

"I'm not really," Graham replied. "I just find pacing hard work."

"This weather isn't going to help," Melanie said and then turned around. "I know I wasn't always your mum's biggest fan, but I'm very worried."

"Well, I won't judge you. I can't imagine living with my mum could've been easy," Graham said as he turned the sound down on the TV.

"Why did you do it? Let her move in I mean? Stuart told me she felt lonely and you were helping her out. But I know my brother well enough to know when he's lying." Graham realized he'd used present tense, but it was too painful to correct, so he let it pass.

Melanie drew a breath like she was going to say something but stopped herself. Then shook her head and said "I might as well tell you. It doesn't matter now anyway." She sat down next to Graham on the sofa. "So, he bought this piece of land a couple of years back. Got it cheap as the seller wanted to get rid of it quickly. Stu was convinced he'd get planning permission on it before selling it on." Melanie paused and wiped the area under her eyes to remove any mascara that might have run. Graham feared it was only going to be moments before she started crying. She took another deep breath and continued "Well, it turned out the land was contaminated with some chemical from the factory that had been there before. And two weeks after he bought it the council served a notice on him to decontaminate the site. He looked into it and it would cost a fortune."

"Didn't the seller know about this?" Graham asked. "Seems a bit of a coincidence that the council would act so soon after the sale?"

"Exactly what Stuart thought," Melanie said looking up at Graham. "He contacted a lawyer to get the sale cancelled and even ended up taking the guy to court. No luck and by this time we'd run out of money."

"So you suggested to Dorene that she could move in with you so you could use the money from selling her house to sort the land out?" Graham said.

"Yes, pretty much. She was very good about it, your mum. And it would only be until we could sell the land on again and then we'd pay her back," Melanie added.

"Well, that explains a lot," Graham said and looked at his phone. Still no news from the police.

"But that wasn't the end of the story," Melanie continued. "The money from the sale of your mum's house wasn't enough, so Stuart ended up getting a loan from a friend of a friend at the golf club to make up the difference. But then, when the clean-up and the sale dragged on, this person demanded his money back and became very threatening." At this point, Melanie couldn't hold the tears back and started crying. Graham felt very awkward and wasn't sure what to do, but gave in to his instinct and put his arm around Melanie. She leant into him and he could smell her shampoo.

She continued the story between blowing her nose and wiping her eyes and Graham found out that Stuart hadn't coped well with the stress of owing money to what had turned out to be a loan shark. He'd become paranoid about the whole affair and had started drinking heavily. At one point he had even stormed into the council offices and accused them of taking bribes. Their relationship had suffered as Melanie had struggled to recognize him as the man she had married only three years earlier. They had put a brave face on it to protect Dorene, who wasn't aware of the money owed, and thought she had saved the situation by selling her house. When they finally had managed to sell the land, they paid off the loan together with the ludicrously high interest. To their relief, Dorene had been happy to move into sheltered accommodation which meant they were able to buy this house. Melanie had emphasized that Stuart had promised that Graham wouldn't be shortchanged when it came to inheriting from his mother and they had planned to tell him what had happened but Stuart had been dragging his feet about it.

After mentioning the inheritance Melanie had started crying heavily once again.

"And then I think I killed him," she whimpered so quietly that Graham had first struggled to hear what she had said.

"What do you mean?" Graham asked as he straightened himself trying to make eye contact with Melanie who was leaning forward with her head in her hands.

"We had a massive fight on Saturday morning," Melanie said as she turned her head and wiped her nose with the sleeve of her merino wool jumper. "I had booked a table at La Dolce Vita for that evening as he'd promised that we could go out for a change. When he was in the presence of others he would still make an effort to be nice, but when we were alone I could barely get him to look at me. He would just mope around. Anyway, on Saturday morning he said he'd changed his mind and didn't want to go and I totally lost it. We had a shouting match and I ended up calling him an egoistic impotent loser and told him that I'd go on my own and that he'd regret not coming as there would be plenty of men who'd love to spend the evening with me. In the end, I just went to see a friend to calm down and didn't go back until late that night." Melanie got off the sofa and went to the kitchen. She came back with a glass of water but didn't sit down again.

"And?" Graham asked. Melanie looked confused. "Why do you think you killed him?" he continued.

"It's obvious, isn't it? You heard Helen. He'd even gone and changed his will that afternoon. And the autopsy taking so long. They must have found some pills in his stomach or something."

"I see," Graham replied. "Did he leave a note?"

"I didn't see one. But maybe it was left outside and blew away?" Melanie answered back.

"But I thought your neighbour said a girl was with him? I didn't want to ask you about it at the time, but surely he wouldn't have killed himself in the company of someone else?" Graham said while trying to get up from the sofa in a graceful manner.

"I wouldn't believe a word of what Helen says. She has been hostile to me from the moment I moved in. Horrible woman. Wouldn't this person, whoever it was, have the decency to stay around if the person they were visiting had just died?" Melanie was getting quite worked up now and Graham was also getting stressed.

Graham wasn't sure what to think. This whole thing just didn't sound like Stuart at all. Suicide or not, he started to feel that he had failed his brother. Last time he'd seen him he had seemed ok, although it was a while ago to be fair. He had been in a far better mood than Melanie anyway. Graham had just assumed Melanie had been a difficult woman to live with, but maybe it had been the other way around. He had always assumed things were going to go well for Stuart, and maybe Stuart had always made the same assumption. Perhaps he'd been too proud to admit he'd made a mistake, presumably since he had never had to deal with failure before. If only he'd let Graham know so he could have offered some support. He wasn't sure in what way, but that somehow didn't matter. Graham felt another lashing of guilt making itself at home in his chest.

Melanie announced that she was going to bed.

He also went to bed but couldn't sleep as his brain was still digesting everything that had happened that day. He felt useless for not being out searching for his mother and guilty for not having realized that his brother had gone through such a bad patch. He was just drifting off when his phone rang. It was the police. They had found Dorene.

9

Dorene found herself sitting with a cup of cold coffee in a garden she didn't recognize. She couldn't recall the reason for her being there. She remembered there being lots of other people with her not long ago and she could see several empty coffee cups on the table in front of her. She put all the cups back on the tray and took them into the kitchen.

The kitchen also looked unfamiliar but she still put the tray down on the counter. She wanted to wash the cups but couldn't see any washing-up liquid or a sponge anywhere. While she looked for them, she became more and more convinced that she must be in the wrong house. How embarrassing. Just imagine if they thought she was a burglar! She'd better leave before anyone saw her.

Dorene let herself out quietly via the front door and continued onto the pavement thinking that Stuart would have a good laugh when she told him about her mistake. She wandered along the street looking at each residence she passed but didn't recognize any of them. Perhaps she shouldn't have left the house after all. She decided to turn around, but even despite inspecting each house carefully she eventually ended up at the entrance to the estate. She tried not to panic. Surely someone will turn up soon so she could ask where Stuart lives. She waited for ages but not a single person appeared.

In the end, she walked out of the estate onto the main road and immediately felt relieved. Opposite the entrance on the other side of a hedge was a white flag on a thing long pole. Of course, that's where Stuart will be. She must have come with him to the golf course and got a bit lost. Could happen to anyone. If only she could get back on the golf course then she'd find him and all would be well. Feeling more positive about her situation she felt the best thing was to aim straight for the flag and squeeze through the hedge. Thankfully the hedge gave way quite easily but a few stray branches of bramble tore at her paper-thin skin on both her hands leaving painful red scratches.

Once through to the fairway, she brushed the leaves and cobwebs off her coat and started walking towards the flag. Suddenly she heard someone shout "Fore!" which made her jump and look around just in time to see a ball coming her way. The ball landed only a meter away from her and the most sensible thing would be to pick it up. It clearly belonged to someone and if it was left in the grass they might never find it. She collected it and put it in her pocket just as two golfers pushing dark blue golf bags in front of them appeared over the brow.

She continued walking around the beautifully kept lawns looking for Stuart, managing to collect another six balls that the golfers had carelessly left lying about. She had just bent down to pick up her seventh ball when a man shouted at her in broad Glaswegian. She couldn't make out what he was saying but he seemed very angry and was walking briskly towards her. As he got closer she could see his bright red face and she became mesmerized by the movements of his large and fleshy mouth and the incomprehensible sounds coming out of it. Fascination turned into fear when he was still screaming at her from less than a meter away. He ripped the ball out of her hand and waved at her to leave. She did as she was told and walked towards the bushes by the side of the nicely mown grass. She could feel tears welling up in her eyes.

She kept following the rough edge of the fairway until she spotted a lake. A bench was positioned next to it and she sat down and watched the Canada geese waddle around pecking in the long grass. Watching the birds calmed her down. A mother with a toddler in reins was doing a circuit of the lake. In her other hand she was pushing an empty buggy with a limping old labrador tied to it. The toddler wanted to stop to look at every pebble and yellow leaf, making for slow progress. Dorene watched as they slowly passed the bench she was sitting on. The dog looked her in the eye with a mix of resignation and recognition as if to say "I might be tied up to a trolley and dragged out for walks with a small imbecile, but at least my family hasn't dumped me in a home".

It started to rain and Dorene had no idea how long she had been sitting on the bench. She stood up and her legs felt cold and stiff. She decided to follow the edge of the golf course back to where she had come from hoping to see Stuart, but at the same time not draw attention to herself. While walking through the increasingly heavy downpour, she eventually got to the large green metal sheds that housed various strange machines. One of the sheds was open fronted so she sought shelter inside hoping the rain might ease off.

She was studying a metal bin full of golf clubs that were either bent or snapped when she saw a man walking towards the back of the clubhouse. That's Stuart, she thought, feeling a surge of happiness. She started following him but lost track as she turned the corner of the house. He must have gone inside, she thought and went up to the only door at the back of the building in the hope she might find her son. She entered and found herself in an unusual-looking kitchen that had three microwaves and two gas hobs. But there were no signs of anyone inside. She was about to leave when she spotted a container of milk left out on the stainless steel worktop. How careless, she thought and started to look around for the fridge. She eventually spotted a large door with a large blue label saying "FRIDGE". That's where they'll keep the fridge then, she thought, as she entered the surprisingly chilly little room. Her wet clothes immediately transferred the cold to her tired body and she felt confused. She looked around but wasn't able to see a fridge anywhere and had started to feel slightly annoyed when suddenly the door behind her closed and the lights went out.

10

Josie was halfway through her shift behind the bar at the golf club when the police turned up together with her manager. Initially, she was shitting herself but felt relieved when she found out they were there to coordinate the search for an old lady that had gone missing. Thankfully there weren't many golfers around as the weather had deteriorated and most had already finished their rounds of golf and gone home, so she kept herself busy by providing teas and coffees to the search parties as they came and went away with new instructions.

She had called in at the golf club the previous evening to double-check that she had the afternoon shift. She had nearly given up hope that she might find her phone, even though she had been back twice to Kilmardinny Gardens without any luck. Last night she had brought a torch with her and searched every inch of the gazebo. It was probably wishful thinking that the phone would still have been there. But she couldn't just knock on the door and ask if someone had found her phone next to the dead man in the hot tub, the one that she may well have killed.

For weeks they had been flirting with each other, her and Stuart. In quite an innocent way to be honest, just like she would flirt with some of the other golfers. Just teasing them a bit. They gave good tips when she got it just right and it made a pretty dull job a bit more exciting. Most of them knew they weren't in her league and that it was just a bit of fun. Stuart was different. He had been in her league and it had made her slightly nervous. She had to confess that she had fallen in love with him slightly and she hated herself for it. The other golfers were like fat roaming beef cattle following the herd around the grassy course, in their uniform of golf club approved clothing. Stuart had seemed so much younger, always tanned and in great shape. He had often been in trouble for changing shirts and shoes in the car park instead of using the locker room as the golf club rules stipulated. She wasn't sure if it was to deliberately show off how fit he was or if he just hated complying with pointless rules. She suspected it was a bit of both and she certainly hadn't minded watching him.

She still couldn't believe what had happened only three days earlier. She had arrived for her Saturday shift at ten in the morning as usual. The unusually sunny weather meant the day was going to be busy and the car park was almost full. It wouldn't be long before players would come back from their rounds, thirsty and keen to have a couple of pints before they had to go home and spend the rest of the day doing the chores set out for them by their wives. When Stuart arrived at eleven there were a loud bunch of middle-aged men at the bar, already on their second pints. He ordered a pint of lager and sat down at the bar at his usual spot by the window overlooking the car park and started reading the newspaper. He hadn't seemed himself and Josie wondered if something had happened. She had been looking for a good moment to ask him, but each time been interrupted. At one point she left the bar area to collect empties from the tables and returned with her hands full of glasses walking past the Lyle and Scott polo shirt brigade. She noticed that they had gone quiet as she passed them but hadn't expected that one of them would smack her on her rear. And a hard smack at that, causing her to jump and lose the grip of the glasses she was carrying. They clattered on the floor with a couple of them breaking. She heard the men laughing and one of them shouted "Hey, we'll get a good view of her arse clearing that mess up, clumsy cow."

She had been utterly unprepared for what had happened. Sure, the odd whistle and ogling she was used to and quite enjoyed, but humiliation, that was a different thing altogether. She still hadn't faced the group as she was contemplating her next move while trying to fight the temptation to just put up with it when suddenly she heard Stuart speak. She turned around just in time to see him shout "You arsehole!" and swing a strong right-handed punch that landed heavily on the red face of a bald man wearing checked trousers and a pullover casually draped over his shoulders.

The man was forced backwards and bent over holding his face. Muffled swear words came out of his mouth together with drops of blood. He straightened up and took a step closer to Stuart, who remained in the same spot, radiating confidence by not even putting his guard up. His friends got off their barstools closing in slightly behind their mate. But none of them acted, scared to be the next victim. The sight of blood soaking in through the lemon yellow fabric of their friend's polo shirt had made them sober up at record speed. They muttered and cursed and left the bar within five minutes, staying just long enough to feel they hadn't escaped in a cowardly fashion. Truth be told, none of them had wanted to risk their wives raising unnecessary questions that could have put a stop to their Saturday morning foray into toxic masculinity.

In the light of what had just happened, she felt obliged to say yes when Stuart asked if she fancied coming over to his house that same evening. She also felt very flattered by the invitation. She wasn't quite sure what he had in mind as she was aware that he was married. She had met Melanie at the golf club several times. Perhaps he just felt sorry for her after what had just happened and wanted to make sure she wasn't on her own that evening. He had left shortly after and the afternoon had been very busy.

After she had got off her shift, she had quickly gone home to shower and change clothes. She wasn't sure about what to wear as it might just be a family dinner with Melanie and perhaps Tom, her brother Jack's best friend, so settled for a pair of white jeans with a teal coloured sleeveless shirt that could be unbuttoned to reveal as much or as little cleavage as appropriate for the situation. She managed to create some nice laid-back curls through her highlighted shoulder-length hair and applied as much makeup she could get away with without looking like she had made too much of an effort. She still lived with her parents but at twenty-two she felt no need to tell them where she was going. She left the house at quarter to eight for the fifteen-minute walk over to the Kilmardinny estate.

Music was coming from inside Eagle's Nest Manor and the front door had been left slightly ajar. She took it as an invitation to let herself in and closed the door behind her. The interior was luxurious with little LED accent lights dotted around the spacious hallway making the house look very inviting. They were no doubt controlled by an app or remote control and must have cost a fair amount to install. She cautiously went through to the lounge, following the sound of the music, but found the room unoccupied and instead returned to the hallway and peered into the large kitchen diner. The dining table hadn't been set. She wasn't sure if that was a good or a bad sign but decided to unbutton the top two buttons of her shirt as she had the distinct feeling that Melanie was not around for the evening. On the table was an open bottle of champagne standing in a pool of condensation. She felt a breeze coming from the open patio doors and walked towards them to take a look outside. Her excitement was gradually being replaced by unease at being alone in a strange house.

"Glad you could make it," she suddenly heard from behind her. She turned around and saw Stuart enter the kitchen carrying a cardboard box. "Just got some more garden lights from the garage," he said, putting the box down on the table. "I'm sure I've got some batteries somewhere," he continued and walked past her to the kitchen, where he opened one drawer after another.

She wasn't quite sure what to do. She was surprised at the informal reception she had received and felt like someone who had accidentally turned up two hours early to a party. Once Stuart had opened and closed all the kitchen drawers without finding what he was looking for, he looked up at her and stopped in his tracks. "Can I get you a drink?" and he gestured towards the bottle on the table. He got a champagne flute out of one of the glass-fronted cupboards and handed it to her. She picked the bottle up but despite its solid weight, only a few drops were left. "Sorry, I'll open another one, hang on." Stuart got a bottle of the same variety out of the fridge. She couldn't help thinking that having several bottles of champagne of the same kind must be a sure sign of wealth. Not like in her house where at best there might be a rabble of various bottles of fizz that people had given them as gifts.

Josie felt more relaxed having a glass of bubbly in her hand, as at least one rule of social etiquette had now been observed. Stuart found a packet of batteries in a plastic tub he'd got out from one of the cupboards and pulled out the tangled mess of fairy lights from the box. He put batteries in a couple of the sets, which made the table light up with a mix of pink flamingos and twinkling stars. It was quickly apparent that trying to fully separate the lights would be a time-consuming task. Instead, he made a large hole in the middle of the spaghetti nest and draped it over Josie's neck. He put his glass up to hers and said "Here's to a bright future!" She quite liked the gesture but wasn't sure how to interpret it. She couldn't read his face well enough to know if it was meant to be a compliment or a joke. He seemed happier than he had been that morning, but there was something resembling desperation in his eyes. She drank another large mouthful from her glass, thinking that whatever happened that evening, being drunk was definitely going to help.

Stuart topped up both their glasses and suggested they go out into the garden. Even though it was dark outside there was residual heat coming from the decking and they sat down next to each other on the steps leading down to the lawn.

They sat in silence for a few minutes, staring into the darkness. Josie could feel the champagne kicking in and realised that it had been a mistake not to eat anything before leaving home.

"Fancy going in the hot tub?" Stuart suddenly asked, then got his phone out and pressed a couple of buttons. The gazebo lit up and she could hear the jets starting up somewhere under the hot tub covers.

"Yeah, ok," Josie answered. Anything was better than awkward silence.

They undressed in the gazebo, Josie one item of clothing behind Stuart to make sure she didn't act presumptuously. She expected each family had their own unwritten rules on what was an acceptable amount of clothing to wear in the hot tub. When Stuart pulled off his boxer shorts and stood naked looking at her, she took her knickers off and quickly got into the water in an act of modesty. She couldn't help noticing that for an older guy Stuart was indeed attractive.

He joined her in the water, sitting down in the

moulded seat next to her so they both could look out over the garden. A moment later he put his arm around her and she knew at that point that something was definitely going to happen and she was nervously looking forward to it. He leaned over, brushed away a strand of hair from her face, and kissed her while the bubbles were drowning out the sound from the outside world. She felt his free hand running over her chest and settling on her left breast.

That's when things started to go downhill.

She felt she should do something in return and decided to place her hand on Stuart's cock. She had expected to feel something firm but after a minute nothing had stiffened up and she had started to feel embarrassed. Stuart suddenly got up and asked her to wait a second. He got out of the tub and she could hear him searching amongst his clothes. When he got back he washed something down with a sip from his champagne and sat down, this time in the seat opposite her in the tub. He reached down and lifted one of her legs up and started to massage her foot and calf. He eventually moved further up her leg and ended up next to her and began gently kissing her ear.

Josie had never seen a naked man without an erection before, something she put down to her own attractiveness, but was probably more to do with the temporary nature of her previous relationships. She felt uneasy and hesitant as she couldn't tell what was going on under the surface because of all the bubbles. She decided to give it all she had and took a deep breath and disappeared into the water. By touch she located what she was aiming for and slipped it into her mouth. It wasn't fully erect but at least there were some signs of activity. She hoped that in the brief time she had at her disposal, she could get it to the state it ought to be in. Her efforts were quickly rewarded and she felt Stuart's body twitching. She kept going until the lack of oxygen made her feel faint, before resurfacing with a big smile on her face.

Stuart's head was slumped forwards. She touched his shoulder but instead of lifting his head, he drew a rather shallow gasp of air. She had been calling his name to get him to respond when the water had suddenly turned light brown in colour, gradually going darker with each passing second. At that point, she screamed in panic and climbed out of the tub.

She knew she had behaved badly by gathering up her clothes and jumping over the fence last Saturday night. She had no idea what had just happened but suspected that if she had declined the offer of spending the evening at Stuart's, none of this would have happened. She hadn't known for sure that Stuart had died until Monday afternoon when she got to the golf club and people had been talking about it at the bar. She had felt like a murderer and still did.

Josie snapped out of her thoughts regarding the previous three days when Melanie walked into the golf club bar area. She felt a surge of adrenaline mixed with guilt and wasn't sure if to offer her condolences or not. Melanie wasn't on her own and the big guy she was with broke the silence by ordering them both drinks. From their conversation, Josie could tell that the missing person was Stuart's mum. This made her feel even more remorseful about what had happened that weekend.

Melanie and the big guy didn't stay very long. After they left, Josie got the chance to return to the kitchen to finish putting together a tray of supplies for making tea and coffee to complement the kettle she had already moved into the room from where the police were running the search. She took the tray across and left it on a table and explained that she was finishing up for the day but the kitchen would be left unlocked should they need anything later.

She returned to the kitchen and noticed that she must have left the walk-in fridge door slightly ajar. She closed it and proceeded to fill in the environmental health checklists before turning off the lights and leaving by the kitchen entrance into the gloomy and wet evening.

11

Graham was half asleep and struggled to make sense of what the policeman was saying on the other end of the line. After the officer had repeated the message several times he finally understood. They had found Dorene inside the walk-in fridge at the golf club and she was alive. She had been taken to Queen Elizabeth Hospital and was being treated for hypothermia and the hospital would get in touch with him shortly with more information. Or at least that is what he thought they had said. He wasn't entirely sure but thanked the officer for all his help anyway. After the phone call, he was left sitting on the edge of the bed not knowing what to do next. He wanted to go to the hospital but had drunk far too much wine to drive and they'd said the hospital would call him. In the end, he laid down on the bed with the bedside light on and waited.

When the phone rang again it pulled Graham out of several layers of unconsciousness and he wasn't quite sure what was happening. The reality finally beat off the dreams that remained in his mind and he quickly sat up and fumbled with the phone, terrified that he'd not be able to answer it in time. When the nurse had finished introducing herself, he had remembered everything from the day before.

"Sorry for not contacting you earlier," she apologized. "The police failed to give us the number for next of kin and it took a little while to track you down." Graham quickly took the phone from his ear and glanced at the time, eight o'clock, he'd been asleep for over five hours.

"Mrs Firth is currently in intensive care. She's lucky to be alive and we aren't sure of the prognosis yet as it is still too early to say. Probably best if you make your way here as soon as you can, so we can give you more information."

Graham said he'd come at once.

He got up, stumbled on the scatter cushions as he tried to retrieve his shirt and trousers from the floor. He took one sniff of the shirt and decided that he'd have to change to the only clean one he had left, even though he had reserved it for Stuart's funeral. He left his room and gently knocked on the door to the master bedroom but there was no response. He went downstairs and found Melanie drinking a glass of orange juice in the kitchen.

"Any news? I've heard nothing," she said before Graham had a chance to tell her about the phone call he'd just received. He gave her the details, omitting the fact that the police had called him earlier in the night.

"Well, we'd better go straight away," Melanie said and put the glass down in the sink. "Your car or mine?"

"Probably yours. My passenger seat is still a bit moist. I've not had a chance to do anything about it after Mum was in it," Graham confessed.

"No problem," Melanie replied and grabbed her handbag from which she fished out the keys to her

Range Rover Evoque. Graham was amazed by how well she looked considering how much they had had to drink the night before. Despite wearing his nicest shirt, he felt like a discarded sofa on a council estate in comparison.

As they walked through the front door a red Jaguar pulled up and parked in front of them.

"Shit," Melanie muttered. "It's Ray, Stuart's accountant. I'd forgotten he was coming." She turned around and closed the door behind her. "He wants to go through Stuart's accounts and the will."

A bald gentleman in a grey suit that looked too shiny to ever be flattering, got out of the car with insincere sympathy and pity written across his face.

"My condolences Mrs Firth, it must have been such a shock for you." He walked up and gave Melanie an unsolicited kiss on her left cheek.

"Yes, it was," she replied, and Graham could see she was tempted to rub her cheek but hesitated as she didn't want to spoil her carefully applied makeup.

"Well, I've brought…" Ray started but was interrupted by Melanie, who in short terms explained what the current situation was and that they would have to reschedule.

"Ok, fine, yes you go to the hospital. Shall I come back tomorrow? The sooner we deal with this the better really. I could bring Dorene's will too if you like?" Ray continued while still standing uncomfortably close to both Melanie and Graham.

"Forgive me, but that seems like jumping the gun," Graham said while taking a step forward, forcing the accountant to shuffle backwards. "We're quite hoping we won't need it just yet," he added and felt quite proud to be acting in a similar way to what Stuart would have done in the same situation. With that as a parting statement, he and Melanie got into the car and pulled out of the drive.

They travelled in silence as neither of the pressing topics seemed suitable to discuss while driving. Graham wondered what the will would reveal. And which will? Was it the new will that the neurotic neighbour had alluded to, or the old one? He had always assumed Stuart was more or less financially independent, but the previous evening's chat with Melanie had made him wonder.

At the hospital, they quickly found a car parking space and made their way to the ICU department. A receptionist told them to sit down in the waiting area until someone was available to talk to them. After a few minutes, Graham said "You don't like Ray much, do you?"

"No, could you tell?" Melanie said and smiled. "He's been Stuart's accountant since the stuff with the land development." Melanie's face had once again turned serious. "According to Stuart, he is good. Or the word he used was innovative. Is that what makes a good accountant? I don't know." Melanie turned and looked towards the reception, hoping that someone was on their way to them soon. "I'll have to give him a ring later. He's right, I'll need to start dealing with things as soon as possible."

"Melanie? I thought you might be coming," said a handsome man carrying a Barbour jacket that had appeared from one of the corridors.

"Mike! So good to see you." Melanie quickly stood up and gave him a hug.

"I'm just about to head home... I was on call last night. I believe I know why you're here. Very unfortunate, but at least there are good signs," he continued.

"Graham, this is Mike, he lives next door," Melanie said in the way of introduction.

"Hi, I'm Graham, Stuart's brother. Nice to meet you. I think I met your wife yesterday," Graham said and shook Mike's hand. He could feel Mike's eyes running him up and down and he was no doubt thinking that surely he and Stuart weren't related.

"I'm so sorry about Stuart. Terrible news, but maybe not totally unexpected," Mike said just as a stocky young man looking no older than about twenty joined them. He was wearing green scrubs and both forearms were tattooed with Norse runes snaking their way up his short-sleeved top and a stethoscope was draped around his neck.

Graham wanted to ask Mike what he had meant by not unexpected but was interrupted by him introducing them to Dr McTavish, who apparently was in charge of Dorene's care. Graham suddenly felt very old.

"I'll leave you in McTavish's capable hands, see you both later," Mike said and left the waiting area.

"Mrs Firth is still unconscious, I'm afraid. It has been touch and go, but we think she is stable now," Dr McTavish explained to them.

"Can we see her?" Graham asked tentatively, as he

didn't really know what else to say.

"Yes, I'll speak to one of the nurses later, but first I'll go through some things with you while you are here." The doctor opened a folder with some notes. "So you know she was severely hypothermic when she was brought in?" he said more as a statement than a question.

"Yes," Graham answered, "we came as soon as we heard."

"Thankfully the police and the rescue teams did the right thing when they found her by very carefully moving her from the fridge to a warmer place. If any of the cold blood from her extremities had migrated to her heart it could have caused a cardiac arrest. She was so severely hypothermic that we've had to put her on an ECMO machine, which has taken over her circulation and will gently warm her blood up. It is too early to say what the prognosis is, but we think there is at least a 50:50 chance she'll pull through. Even if she does, we won't know what the effects on her brain and other organs might be. Sorry for sounding pessimistic, but I don't want to give you false hope. You must realize she is in a very serious condition."

Graham was trying so hard to concentrate on what the doctor was saying that he missed half of it. Suddenly Melanie was tugging at his arm saying "Graham, the doctor's asking about her medical history."

"Yes, do you know what medication Mrs Firth is on?" the doctor asked patiently, clearly used to people not being fully together.

"No, I'm not sure," Graham said, "but I can go back

to the house to check. Pretty sure she'll have brought any medicines with her."

"Don't worry, we are requesting her notes, so we'll get the information soon anyway. But apart from her dementia, does she suffer from any other health problems?"

"No, I don't think so," was the only answer Graham could manage as his mind felt totally blank.

"Right, wait here and I'll try and arrange for you to see her."

Dr McTavish wandered off to reception and soon a cheerful dark-haired nurse approached them. "Please come with me," she said and made a gesture towards one of the corridors.

Graham and Melanie followed the nurse and after a few turns along pastel-coloured corridors, that all looked the same, they arrived in a treatment room that looked like a space shuttle control centre. There were instruments with dials and displays showing numbers and traces, which occasionally beeped. Clear bags with liquids that were either going in or out were hanging on stands next to the bed. In the middle was the contour of a very small and frail-looking body.

Everything became too much for Graham and he could feel tears building up in his eyes. Melanie noticed. Feeling her embrace unlocked the floodgates to all the tension that had built up over the last few days and he stopped trying to hold back his tears.

12

Helen told Mike she'd prepared a cooked breakfast for him when he arrived back home. She knew she'd only have an hour or so before he would go to bed for a few hours' rest after the night shift. She wanted to talk about the police turning up at next door's the previous day, a clear sign, in her mind, that there had been something suspicious about Stuart's death.

She greeted him with a kiss, but her cheerful mood drained away instantly when she again could smell the sweet scent of vanilla on his neck. She muttered that breakfast was warming in the oven and went upstairs to the bathroom. To say she slammed the door behind her would have been exaggerating, but she certainly closed the door more forcefully than normal. She sat down on the toilet and tried to calm down from the rage that was growing inside her. Stuart wasn't even buried yet, how could he? And how could Melanie?

She didn't want to show Mike her anger so decided to have a shower to prolong the time she could hide in the bathroom. When she finally went downstairs, to her great relief there was an empty plate on the table and no Mike. She took the opportunity to go out to check the mileage on Mike's car, feeling transformed from the unreasonable suspicious wife to a woman who was collecting evidence with which to confront her lying partner. The mileage had only increased by the exact distance of a return trip to the hospital.

Instead of feeling disappointed that she hadn't got any proof, she felt relief. She suddenly realized she didn't want to leave Mike but at the same time, she was acutely aware of how weak and pathetic she was. She hated it that even if he betrayed her, she would just put up with it, like a coward. Again. Maybe she could confront Mclanic about it? To make her realize that she wasn't letting her have Mike without a fight. That way Mike would never need to know about her knowing and it wouldn't be an issue between them. The more she thought about it, the more she liked the idea. Best not confront Melanie personally though, not to start with anyway. She had enjoyed creating yesterday's little scene. But hinting at something wasn't the same as making actual threats. Also, Helen didn't feel she had the right persona to intimidate someone with violence in person. Instead, she decided to write a note that she could post through the letterbox. Keeping it anonymous just in case she was wrong. She was good at notes. If Melanie decided to go to the police, she wouldn't be able to prove that it was Helen who had written the letter.

When Mike got up three hours later, he found Helen in a surprisingly cheerful mood. There was an energy there that had been lacking in recent days. She seemed eager to talk about something, but he had to shoot off as he had several patients to see at the hospital that afternoon.

13

Josie arrived at the golf club the next morning and was greeted by the young Asian and the ginger female police officer from the day before. They wondered if they could ask her a few questions. She unlocked the main door, went inside, and switched a few of the lights on. It was a gloomy day. She assumed that they had found out she had been at Stuart's house the night he'd died and she was trying to buy herself some time to figure out what to tell them.

She offered them a table and they sat down together. The male officer took the lead and told her that Dorene, the lady they had been searching for yesterday, had been found. Both officers were staring at her and she realised they were waiting for her reaction.

"That's great news, isnae it?" she said.

"She is in a very serious condition in hospital," the officer added, again waiting for her to reply. What's this got to do with me, Josie thought.

"Oh, that's a shame," she said in the hope that more information might be made available.

"Do you know where we found her?" came the next question and Josie started to feel quite nervous.

"No, should ah?" she replied, trying to hide her fear.

"Apart from yourself, who had access to the kitchen

yesterday?" the ginger female officer asked.

Josie's thoughts went back to the previous day. She remembered now. The door to the walk-in fridge being open and her closing it without looking inside. Woah? No, surely not. Another wave of adrenalin swept through her body, a feeling that was now becoming familiar to her.

"Do I have to repeat the question?" the police officer said impatiently.

"Ah'm trying tae think," Josie replied. "The outside door's always left unlocked so the ground staff can get tea and coffee. Sometimes they put their lunchboxes in the walk-in fridge. So I suppose anyone could've entered the kitchen yesterday." Josie felt pleased with her answer. It spread the suspicion onto a number of people, not just her.

The rest of the conversation revolved around who was responsible for the health and safety checks on the premises and why nobody had discovered that the door handle on the inside of the fridge was broken. Josie felt that most of the blame could legitimately be put on her manager, which made her feel better, at least temporarily.

The officers left just before the first golfer turned up at the bar and Josie spent the rest of the day feeling terrible. What would Tom think if he ever found out that she probably had killed his dad and maybe his Nan as well?

14

At the nurses' station, Melanie and Graham were reassured that someone would contact them immediately if anything changed. Graham started to walk towards the exit and realised that Melanie wasn't following him. He turned around and saw her still standing by the now empty counter, staring into space. She suddenly came alive and quickly joined him.

"Sorry, I was miles away," she said as they approached the exit of the ICU department. "I just realized that Stuart will be somewhere in this huge building. I just can't get my head around it."

"Do you want to ask if you can go and see him? To say goodbye?" Graham offered.

"No, I said goodbye last Saturday. But you kind of think that after you say goodbye, they should just be gone. But he is still here. Somewhere. Just feels weird that's all." Melanie linked her arm with his and he felt both scared and flattered at the same time.

"Come on, let's go for lunch," Melanie suggested. "I know a Greek place that does wonderful coffee."

"Sounds great." Not only was Graham very hungry but he was also acutely aware of his stale breath due to the lack of breakfast and the fact he'd not even had time to brush his teeth that morning after an evening of heavy drinking.

After a short drive, they arrived at a place that was far from the cosy taverna that Graham had imagined. It boasted double-height floor-to-ceiling windows. The gloomy day made the interior designer light pendants sparkle and the waiters were smartly dressed in white shirts and black waistcoats. Many tables were already filled, mainly with couples, and they were all looking at Graham and Melanie as they entered. Graham was grateful for wearing his best shirt, but still felt very uncomfortable.

"Madame. Sir... Table for two?" the head waiter enquired with a suitably strong Greek accent. He looked remarkably similar to George Clooney and Graham took an immediate dislike to him.

"Yes please." Melanie quickly answered and they were shown to a table near the bar.

Graham looked suspiciously at the fragile-looking designer chair presented to him by the waiter. "Could you point the way to the gents' please?" he asked, buying some time before potentially causing furniture-related embarrassment. He looked at Melanie apologetically and set off towards the back of the restaurant.

While washing his hands, he realized that he'd totally forgotten about Tom and quickly got his phone out and dialled Tom's number. It rang out for a good thirty seconds before a sleepy voice answered with a "Huh?" He filled Tom in on the events that morning with as much optimism as possible without feeling that he was lying. When Graham told him he was having lunch with Melanie in town, Tom asked him if he could come along. He'd never been to a funeral before and his mum had given him some money to buy something nice to wear. Maybe Graham could help him decide what to get? Helping someone buy clothes wasn't something Graham felt qualified to do, but of course he couldn't say no.

Returning to the table, he found Melanie on her phone. Grateful for the distraction he gently lowered himself on the chair, making sure the weight was placed as symmetrically as possible. Despite a bit of creaking the delicate chair seemed to take his weight ok.

Melanie finished the call and put the phone on the table.

"Hope you don't mind but I've already ordered. I've got you the same as me, a large Greek salad. They're excellent here." Melanie said and poured Graham some sparkling Perrier water. Graham tried his best to hide his disappointment. She then announced that Ray, the accountant, was coming the next morning at ten. Her phone rang again and Graham was left hungrily observing the dishes being brought out from the kitchen to waiting diners.

Forty-five minutes later Tom met Graham outside the restaurant and they said goodbye to Melanie and walked towards the main shopping street. Tom seemed to have decided on a shop he wanted to go into so Graham followed him.

"Do you think I should buy a suit?" he asked Graham, while looking at some folded-up grey hoodies placed on a table near the entrance.

"What did your mum say?" Graham answered.

"Not much, she just gave me £100 and told me to come home with something suitable." Tom looked up at Graham and grinned. "Does that mean a suit?"

"Have you got some proper shoes? Something other than trainers I mean," Graham enquired back.

Tom shook his head.

"Smart trousers then?"

"Yes, I've got my old school uniform trousers. They 're black, if that's what you mean?" Tom said.

Three different shops and an hour later Tom was equipped with a shiny pair of black shoes, a black slim-fit shirt, a black tie, and a charcoal grey jumper that Graham paid for as the budget hadn't quite stretched that far.

They took the bus back to Kilmardinny Gardens, but not before stopping at a supermarket where Graham picked up the ingredients for a lasagna and some beers. He wasn't sure Melanie would approve of a meat and gluten-based dish so added some avocados and Quorn to the shopping basket.

When Tom and Graham came through the door to Eagle's Nest Manor, the first thing they saw was a near empty bottle of gin on the kitchen table with an ashen-faced Melanie staring through the patio doors at the garden, holding a large tumbler.

"You won't believe this," Melanie said before emptying the contents of her glass in one sweep. "They are going to re-do Stuart's autopsy."

15

The news of Stuart's second autopsy wasn't the only thing that had driven Melanie to pour herself a large gin with a dash of tonic. It wasn't even the worst thing. The coroner's secretary had explained that repeating an autopsy wasn't uncommon and wasn't necessarily due to any suspicious circumstances. Last time it was due to the pathologist having spilled a cup of coffee over their laptop, which had caused the loss of the data they required to write up the report.

"And frankly, sometimes I think the hospital just says this when they have forgotten to do the autopsy in the first place," she added to comfort Melanie, who had sounded noticeably shaken up. "Don't worry, we'll be in touch when it is all sorted, but I wouldn't plan on arranging the funeral before next week if I were you."

The far worse thing that had upset Melanie was the letter that had been waiting for her on her return from lunch in town. There was no stamp and no address on it. "To Melanie" had been written on the envelope in handwriting that could have belonged to a 3-year-old. Melanie couldn't recall any young children who would want to send her a letter, as she opened the envelope and pulled out a sheet of pale blue paper. The terrible handwriting continued. This time with even smaller letters which made it harder to read.

"*I know what you are doing. Stop immediately otherwise there will be consequences. Think of Stuart. I will be watching you.*"

Melanie paced back and forward. This was definitely not a letter from a child. The person had probably had written it using their left hand or something. Her thoughts immediately went to Stuart's connections within the loan shark underworld. She remembered the time when a bearded Eastern European man, wearing a black bomber jacket, had turned up at their old house. She had opened the door and when he had asked to see Stuart she'd immediately known why he was there. She never knew what the man had threatened him with, but the episode had changed Stuart noticeably and was one of the reasons they had moved away. She had assumed that they had put most of that stuff behind them now. But maybe not? *Think of Stuart.* The possibility that Stuart had actually been murdered no longer seemed like such a farfetched idea and was compounded by the fact that she'd now been told about the second autopsy. She suddenly felt very scared.

But what did she need to stop doing? She had absolutely no idea. She was going through one possibility after another. Was it because someone thought she was spending too much money? Spending money and drinking too much were the only two things she felt she should cut down on. But unless AA had drastically changed the way they recruited new members, the letter was more likely referring to her spending habits. Had the loan sharks started circulating around her now Stuart was dead? Perhaps he was still paying them and now they were worried they weren't going to get their money. She did admit to spending quite a bit recently as she thought she and Stuart might be heading for a divorce, so why not use the money while it was still there.

Or was someone blaming her for what had happened to Dorene? And actually, she wasn't entirely guilt-free as she hadn't supervised her adequately. But how could she have known that Dorene would get lost and end up in a fridge? Not exactly a foolproof plan if you wanted to see someone dead. Also, she had no guarantee that she had anything to gain from Dorene being dead as the financial arrangements were too complicated and Stuart's death would have changed everything anyway. So where was the motive? It just didn't make sense. I will be watching you. Well, watch me drink a large gin then, she thought to herself and poured a large second helping of gin and sat down looking out through the patio doors.

When Graham came back with Tom in tow, Melanie immediately felt better. She had to confess he never entered her thoughts normally, as in her mind he was just Stuart's boring and unsuccessful brother. And she had never found Graham's company particularly stimulating. He was just the unlucky one who hadn't been blessed with good looks or a go-getter attitude. However, in the last twenty-four hours she had come to value his presence and especially his calmness. She wondered if he was calm because of his size or his size made him calm. Or maybe the two things weren't related. She realized she didn't actually know anything at all about him, as every conversation they had ever had, had revolved around her and of course Stuart. She made a mental note to ask him if he subscribed to any philosophical school of thought in the way he lived his life. Although in reality she probably was more interested in knowing if he had ever had a girlfriend. Perhaps he was even still a virgin?

Graham could tell that Melanie must have had quite a bit of gin, so suggested she'd go and lie down while he cooked dinner, an offer which she happily accepted. When dinner was ready Melanie was fast asleep, so Graham and Tom ate on their own. Graham put the Quorn version of the lasagne in the fridge. Tom's conversation seemed to be limited to films they had both watched and Graham was content with that. He was trying to pay just enough attention not to hurt Tom's feelings, but most of his thoughts revolved around the events of the day, and especially around the comment Mike had made around why Stuart's death hadn't been a surprise. Maybe that is what he says to all his deceased patients' relatives to subconsciously lower their expectations and avoid anyone questioning the care they had received at the hospital? But it just didn't make much sense.

Melanie was still asleep when they both went to bed at ten o'clock.

16

Graham woke from a long and restful sleep and sat on the bed for a while before standing up. The grey weather from the previous day had cleared and the morning sun was streaming through the windows. Even the scatter cushions had been beaten back and formed a neat line along the base of the wall. For once he might not trip over them. He cursed himself for not having washed any of his shirts the night before, or even bought a new one while he was shopping with Tom. His only option was to fish out the shirt he had travelled up in from his bag. Not the freshest, but at least it had had a couple of days' rest. He gathered up his dirty clothes and went downstairs.

Melanie was on the phone to the funeral directors, judging by the discussion regarding dates and organists. He was wondering whether to interrupt her to say that if push comes to shove he might be able to play something at the service, but decided against it. He went to the kitchen and put the kettle on and then to the utility room, where he stuffed his clothes in the washing machine and spent several minutes trying to find the cupboard that contained the washing powder.

"Have you heard from the hospital this morning?" he asked Melanie when he returned to the dining area.

"Yes, I phoned them up first thing. No change. She's

still unconscious. And then I phoned the funeral directors to see what availability they have for the end of next week," she replied.

Graham imagined that if Stuart had been there he would probably have joked with Melanie about wanting a two-for-one offer on burials.

"Or do you think we should try and wait a bit longer so that Dorene might be able to come?" she asked Graham.

"Hmm, hard to know. Perhaps coming out of a coma just in time for your son's funeral may not be ideal. I think it's probably kindest not to wait."

"I think you might be right," Melanie agreed.

While Melanie went upstairs to try and get Tom out of bed in time for Ray's arrival, Graham finished his cup of tea.

At quarter past ten the doorbell rang and Melanie let Ray in. They all gathered in the living room with Ray taking the large armchair and dragging the glass coffee table towards him so he could put his briefcase on it. He looked up at them both and asked "No new developments on Mrs Firth's state of health? She's still with us, is she?"

Graham and Melanie both nodded. Tom was staring at his phone.

"Would've made it easier in a way if she wasn't. Sorry to sound crass," Ray said like he thought it was a funny joke. "You see, Dorene had given Stuart lasting power of attorney. So who is going to act on Dorene's behalf now? And with the house partly in her name. Well, you can see the issues, can't you?" Ray said it like he was blaming them for the increase in inconvenience that had been put upon him.

Graham was amazed by how quickly he was developing a strong dislike of Ray.

"And while we are on the topic of Dorene, is the house going on the market soon? The care home has been in touch again and asked for an update on the matter. Melanie?" Ray added and flipped the lid of his suitcase open.

"Yes, we had it valued by the estate agent last week so I expect it will happen very soon. Stuart was the one arranging it all, so I'm not sure what else needs to be done," Melanie said uncomfortably.

Tom and Graham both looked at each other and it was clear neither of them had heard about this until now.

"Anyway," Ray continued, "just as well we rescheduled because when I got back to the office yesterday there was a letter from Stuart waiting for me." He looked quizzically at Melanie. "Did you know he changed his will on the day he died?"

"I didn't until three days ago," Melanie said cautiously.

"Well, I don't deal with wills that often, but I do think it is worth checking that everything is in order and it has been witnessed properly, especially as the death occurred so soon after making the changes," Ray continued. At this point, even Tom was sitting up straight and paying attention.

"As the witnesses both live next door would you mind if I called in and asked them to verify their signatures before we proceed?" Ray said, holding a brown envelope in his hand.

"Not at all, please go ahead," Melanie replied, looking noticeably anxious.

Ray went off and left the three of them sitting in silence. Tom returned to scrolling through messages on his phone and Melanie eventually got up and started pacing backwards and forwards.

It didn't take long before Ray returned and announced that the will was indeed valid and that meant that he, as an executor of the will, would have to make sure Stuart's wishes were followed.

"So, both the old and the new will says that you, Melanie, is entitled to the house, or more specifically, the share of the house that Dorene doesn't own," Ray chuckled. "I think Stuart had forgotten that we put that part in your name already. You know, to protect the house from any claims related to Stuart's business dealings." Ray looked up at Melanie who slowly nodded. "However, when I last checked, it didn't look like you had been paying much off the mortgage in the last 18 months. Not that it is my business, but let's hope you get a good price when you sell it, shall we?" Ray added smugly.

"It also says that Tom," and Ray looked up at Tom to check that he was listening, "is still entitled to all Stuart's other assets on the condition that he gets himself a job or graduates from university. I'm not a solicitor, but even I know that putting these sorts of clauses in a will is not particularly helpful and not likely to be enforced. But before you get your hopes up Tom, it isn't going to be a particularly large sum we are talking about here. Your father still had quite a few debts, such as the cost of the funeral, my own fees, and there hasn't been a lot of money coming in recently. So that leaves us with the new requests that were added to the will." At this point, Ray turned to Melanie and asked "Any chance of a coffee?" A request not many people would make from someone looking daggers at them, other than to infuriate them even more.

Graham swiftly offered to make Ray a coffee as he didn't trust Melanie not to lace it with rat poison, judging by the expression on her face. He returned with a cup of weak lukewarm instant decaf coffee in his own act of rebellion. He had to thank Ray for being the first person he'd met that he felt absolutely no desire to please. It was a liberating experience and he suddenly felt more confident. He watched Ray take a sip of the coffee and wince before putting it on the table and carrying on reading the will.

"Graham," Ray paused melodramatically, "it says here that you are to have the Steinway piano." Both Tom and Melanie nodded approvingly. Graham couldn't help thinking that the piano surely still belonged to Dorene and wasn't for Stuart to give away, but decided not to raise the issue because he was more than delighted that it would finally be in his possession.

"The next request is a bit unusual." Again, Ray paused and adjusted his tie to keep them on tender hooks. Graham thought that Ray must really be enjoying himself.

"It says here that someone called Josie Simmonds should be given his ashes, to be scattered in his favourite hole." Ray looked up at each one of them in turn for clarification. "Does anyone know who Josie Simmonds is? And do we know what kind of hole he is referring to?" Both Melanie and Graham looked at each other trying to process what had just been read out and Graham was on the verge of asking Ray to repeat it when Tom broke the silence.

"I think I know who Josie Simmonds is. It's my mate Jack's older sister. She works at the golf club."

There was a sigh of relief from Melanie and Graham but Ray looked disappointed. It was clear he had hoped for a more compromising revelation possibly requiring him personally to look into the matter. Feeling somewhat shortchanged, he asked Tom "And do you have a number so we can get in touch with her by any chance?"

"No, but I can ask Jack for it." Tom's thumb repeatedly pressed the screen and a few seconds later his phone responded with a ping. "Do you want me to call her?"

"Why not, we might as well find out now whether she is prepared to meet Stuart's request," Ray said, still hoping there might be some embarrassing secrets to discover.

Tom pressed the call button and they waited silently. Tom heard it first, but then both Melanie and Graham looked up too. In the far distance, you could hear a phone ringing. Tom quickly hung up and the sound stopped.

"Tom, what is going on?" Melanie asked as Tom left the living room and ran up to his bedroom.

Outside, a white ford escort van pulled up and a man carrying a for sale sign approached one of the gate posts of Eagle's Nest Manor.

17

Helen had taken great care when writing the anonymous letter. She wore disposable gloves and as a precaution, she ironed the sheet of paper and the envelope in the hope that any previous fingerprints might melt away. It had taken a long time for her to formulate what she wanted to say. She didn't want it to be too obvious in case Melanie went to the police. But at the same time, she wanted to send a clear signal.

After Mike had gone back to work, she snuck over to Melanie's house and posted the letter through the letterbox, feeling strong and empowered. She knew she'd have to keep an eye on Mike and start thinking about the consequences if Melanie didn't obey her demands. She wasn't quite sure what would be appropriate, but thought that the first stage might at least involve dog turds. She had used the dog turd strategy successfully before. More serious actions could be saved for later.

When Mike came home that evening, she had prepared a chicken casserole and opened a bottle of wine. She had even applied some makeup. Mike seemed tired, but she made the effort to keep up a cheerful and engaging conversation nevertheless. She was careful not to mention the police presence next door as the last thing she wanted was to draw attention to Melanie, even though she was desperate to get Mike's opinion on what was happening. After watching TV for an hour they went to bed and made love. She found it hard to switch off enough to have an orgasm, but made up for it by making sure Mike's needs were comprehensively seen to.

The next morning, Helen spotted the for-sale sign going up next door. "My word," she said to herself, "that letter must have hit the spot!"

18

Tom entered his bedroom and quickly located the pink iPhone. Sure enough, his own number was shown as a missed call on the screen. He sat down on the bed and thought about what he should do next. He certainly didn't want to tell anyone that he had found the phone next to the hot tub. He couldn't think why Josie would even have been near the hot tub in the first place.

He messaged Jack to see if he was at home. "YEAH" came the reply. He let Jack know that he was on his way over. He grabbed his black Diesel jacket and put the two phones in the inside pocket and headed for Jack's house.

He didn't bother ringing the doorbell, as in the past no one ever heard it or at least never did anything about it. It had always been a very noisy household with at least one of the three kids playing loud music. It used to be Josie, followed by Jack when he hit puberty, and now the mantle had fallen on Josh, who had just turned fifteen. Josh must be at school as the house seemed pretty quiet, Tom thought as he walked through the door. As usual, the hallway was full of randomly scattered trainers and Tesco shopping bags, containing everything from empty batteries waiting to be taken to the recycling, to remnants of packed lunches from weeks ago.

Tom tiptoed across and went up the stairs to Jack's bedroom. Usually he'd find Jack in bed, but this time he was up and dressed and was packing a backpack with a couple of bottles of Lucozade and a blanket.

"Awricht, shagger. Ah'm sorry aboot yer Da'. Fancy comin' picking some mushies?" Jack grinned at him with gappy teeth and a face covered in freckles. His left ear looked red and angry and Tom suspected he must have had another piercing put in.

Since the commiserations seemed to have been dealt with, Tom just answered yes. Picking magic mushrooms was more or less a tradition and normally the highlight of September. Last year it had even earned them quite a bit of money. Tom's bike was at his mum's, so he borrowed Josie's bike and he and Jack rode off towards the dams, in the hope that someone else hadn't found their favourite spot.

After a while, they had to stop to shed a layer of clothing. The sun had some warmth in it and there was hardly any wind. When they eventually ran out of track, they dumped the bikes behind a stone wall and continued on foot up a grassy hill on the edge of the moorland. Jack started walking more slowly and frequently bent over to get a good look at the grass. Tom did the same but had to admit his heart wasn't quite in it. It didn't take Jack long to spot a beige thin mushroom. He got down on his haunches and separated the grass until he found a few more.

Tom had expected him to start picking them, but instead Jack got the picnic blanket out and spread it on the ground and sat down. Tom sat down next to him.

"What'd ye think of the ket?" Jack asked and got a bottle of Lucozade out of his backpack.

Tom hadn't expected this question since he had been focussed on Josie's phone and been waiting for an opportunity to bring the subject up. He remained silent but eventually said "I've not got around to trying it yet." It wasn't a lie but not the full truth either.

"Have you tried it?" he then asked Jack.

"Fuck no. Way too hardcore for me!" Jack exclaimed and the cheeky grin returned. "I was hoping ye'd be able to tell me if it was any good!"

Tom couldn't tell if Jack was joking.

"Anyhow, keep hold the bag for now. Two polis knocked on my door yesterday. I nearly shat a brick! Turned out they were lookin' tae huckle Josie and no' me." Jack took a big swig of energy drink and then held the bottle out for Tom.

Tom shook his head. This was the opportunity he was waiting for. "Do you know if Josie has lost her phone?"

"What? Did ye not get hold of her yesterday?" Jack asked, looking puzzled. "What did ye want her for anyway?"

"You sure you gave me the right number?" Tom queried.

"Ye wanted her number so I gave it ye," Jack replied, unable to hide his irritation.

At this point, Tom fished out Josie's phone from his coat pocket and handed it to Jack. "I found her phone in my Dad's garden. Maybe you could give it back to her?"

"Sure," Jack replied with a confused look on his face.

"Are we picking mushies or not?" Tom said, relieved that he'd got the phone thing over and done with.

Turned out Jack wasn't planning on taking any mushrooms home with him that day. The visit by the police had freaked him out and he'd even flushed the weed he had stashed under his mattress down the loo, just in case. Instead, he wanted to eat the liberty caps there and then and have one hell of an experience to celebrate the end of summer.

It only took Tom and Jack twenty minutes to gather around forty little mushrooms. It was hard to stop picking them once you got started and often Tom had thought that he enjoyed collecting them more than actually using them. He certainly wasn't in the right mood for psychedelics as his life seemed more surreal than any bad trip he'd ever had.

They sat down on the blanket with their haul. Jack wasn't unhappy about Tom not wanting to participate. "Please yirsel! Aw the mair for me. Just ye make sure ah don't go and dae anythin' mental like shaggin' a sheep or something!" Jack put a handful of mushrooms in his mouth. They were pretty chewy and it took a while until Jack had managed to grind his way through all forty of them.

Jack gave Tom the second bottle of Lucozade and they were chatting about this and that for a good half an hour before Jack started giggling. The laughter was contagious and Tom couldn't help joining in even though he hadn't eaten any mushrooms.

After a while, they laid down and lapped up the warm autumn sunshine like a couple of lizards on hot rocks. High clouds moved across the blue sky, shifting shapes as they did so. Jack started singing a little song to himself as Tom's mind started to wander.

"Was Josie out Saturday night?" Tom asked and turned his head to see Jack with his finger in the air tracing the outline of a floating cloud.

"Probably," came the answer followed by another giggle.

"Do you know where she went?" Tom asked but didn't get a reply. Jack seemed to be in a different place now. After ten minutes of silence, when Tom had started to drift off, Jack suddenly said: "She must have gone to fuck yer Da'."

Tom sat up on his elbows and looked at Jack. "What do you mean?" he asked.

"Yeah, the paedo Da'. The lecherous, creepy, paedo Da' of yers. It's obvious isnae it. I can't believe ah didnae see it before." Jack was still lying down and had put both arms behind his head. "How does it feel to be the son of a paedo? The paedo-child…" Jack lost himself in a laughing fit.

Tom felt the anger brewing inside him. Jack was a bit of a tosser, particularly when drunk or when having taken drugs. He didn't know what Josie had done or if she even had been at his dad's that Saturday, but his dad was not a paedophile. Tom stood up and started walking away.

"Screw you! I hope you do shag a sheep!" he shouted back to Jack.

He walked back to the bike and started to cycle back. He was hoping he might think of a plausible story to tell Melanie and Graham to explain why Josie's phone had been in his bedroom.

19

Ray was telling Melanie about the finer details regarding inheritance tax when Graham's phone rang. It was the hospital asking him if he could come to the ICU department as soon as possible. The news was good. Dorene had been disconnected from the ECMO and had woken up but was slightly agitated. They thought seeing a familiar face might calm her down, so Graham said he'd come straight away.

He interrupted Ray to deliver the news and left Melanie to wrap things up. When he got to the hospital all the car parks looked full. He drove around for a few minutes, but eventually gave up and started to look for a space on the roads near the hospital. He finally managed to park nearly half a mile away. Conscious about the time it would take him to get to Dorene, he started to jog back towards the hospital. He couldn't remember the last time he had had to run and it wasn't in the least bit pleasant. After less than a minute he considered abandoning the attempt. He could feel drops of sweat rolling down his spine and his thighs were sore from chafing. Not to mention how out of breath he felt. His shirt had worked its way out of his trousers and he could feel the cold wind hitting the lower half of his stomach which seemed to be swinging back and forwards hanging over the waist of his trousers. He stopped to catch his breath and saw his reflection in the window of the terraced house next to him. What a sight. He tucked his shirt back into his trousers and started walking slowly to the hospital hoping that his face might take on less of a beetroot colour by the time his mum saw him. Looking like he'd run a marathon would definitely not count as a familiar face.

"She is a true fighter, your mum," said the nurse who took him to Dorene, who had been moved up a floor to a ward above the ICU department. She had improved amazingly quickly and was sitting up when Graham walked up to her bed. She looked immensely relieved when she saw Graham, a feeling that was mutual.

"Graham," she said and Graham was grateful that she recognized him as he had feared the worst, "I think I must have had a funny turn," she continued. "This is such a funny hospital you know." She quickly looked around to make sure nobody was listening. "They all seem to have decided to speak with Scottish accents. How peculiar!"

Graham sat down on the bed and told her what had happened. He decided not to mention Stuart's death. It would probably come back to her when she was ready, now was not the time. They held hands in silence for a long time and eventually Dorene started to drift off. Graham put her thin veiny hand gently on the bed and left to find someone who could tell him what would happen next. He spoke to a nurse, who managed to find the doctor in charge of Dorene's care and Graham was told that Dorene could probably go home the day after, as long as she had someone with her at all times. It would also be good if he could bring along a set of clothes for her to travel home in as the clothes she had been brought in with were no longer intact. They had been forced to cut through them to be able to administer her care.

He felt cheerful as he drove back, pleased to be able to pass on the good news, until he remembered that Dorene surviving would in fact render Melanie homeless. His mood returned to what could best be described as cautiously content when he realised that Melanie would probably be homeless regardless, since it wasn't likely Dorene had mentioned her in her own will anyway.

When he got back to Eagles Nest Manor, Tom was in the kitchen standing on a chair searching the cupboard above the integrated fridge.

"There's never anything to eat in this house!" he exclaimed as he got down and put the chair back at the dining table.

"There's probably some Quorn lasagne in the fridge from yesterday?" Graham said, trying to sound helpful. He could tell that Tom was in a foul mood.

"I want proper food," came a sultry reply, more suited to a three-year-old than an eighteen-year-old.

Graham opened the fridge and the lasagne was where he had put it last night. He hadn't expected Melanie to have had it, she seemed to live on fruit juices, salads, and coffee from what he could gather. He took the dish and placed it in the microwave. When it was warm he plated up two big portions, one for himself and one for Tom. He took the plates to the living room where Tom was watching a football game and gave him a plate. They both ate in silence.

Just as the match finished, Melanie arrived home with some shopping bags. Tom went into the hallway and grabbed a large bag of prawn cocktail flavour crisps from the top of one of the bags, muttered a thank you and went up to his room.

Graham recounted the visit to the hospital while helping Melanie unpack and was fascinated by the products she had bought. He had to read the label of a few just to find out what they were. He'd never encountered things like freekeh and nutritional yeast before. He picked up yet another unusual-looking thin packet and turned it over and realised it was a pregnancy test. He quickly put it back in the bag and instead picked up a tub of vegan Marigold stock powder. Feeling that helping Melanie put away the groceries had become personally intrusive, he made his excuses and left the kitchen. He returned to watching TV and was quickly immersed in watching a man rescue a sheep from a pothole somewhere in Yorkshire.

Melanie went upstairs for a shower and came down looking very different. He initially thought it could have been the natural glow of pregnancy that people always seemed to refer to, but then realized it was the first time he'd seen Melanie without makeup. She walked into the kitchen and returned with a large gin and tonic. "Do you want one?" she asked Graham and he politely declined. "I got some beers as well, just help yourself from the fridge whenever you want. You'd better not leave it too long as Tom will drink them all," Melanie chuckled.

She did seem to be in a good mood, but how that was related to having bought a pregnancy test and holding a large gin and tonic Graham wasn't sure and he decided not to think about it, but assumed that the test had probably been negative. There was too much going on anyway for Graham to worry about Melanie's potential perimenopausal symptoms.

* * *

Later that evening Melanie got busy in the kitchen preparing a Greek meal. Graham was hoping it consisted of more than a salad but felt it would be rude to ask. Tom came down and joined Graham, who was still enjoying watching TV. As expected he immediately asked if he could change channels and normally Graham would have said yes, but he really wanted to see the end of the programme about using classical music to treat army dogs suffering from PTSD, so politely asked Tom to wait.

Tom got his phone out and kept asking Graham questions such as: Are you on Facebook? Snapchat? Instagram then? To which Graham shook his head while still trying to concentrate on the TV. Tom continued by asking if Graham had a website? Or was a member of any online forums? Again Graham shook his head hoping Tom would get the hint that he wasn't interested. Then finally Tom asked if he even had an email. To which Graham nodded.

"What? So the only thing you use is email?" Tom chuckled. "You're like an ex-SAS person trying to remain incognito or something!"

Graham couldn't think of anything more unlikely. Tom stood up and used his phone to take a photo of Graham. "I'll find you. You must be somewhere on the web." He sat down and put the photo into Google. Within a few seconds, Tom was rolling around on the floor laughing. Even Melanie came into the living room to see what was going on, but since Tom was in no fit state to say anything, she left. Eventually, Tom managed to stop laughing for long enough to text the link to Graham.

"Is this really you?" he then asked Graham, who was in the process of opening the link. What Graham saw was a video of a guy looking identical to himself, with no top on, sitting on a sofa and crushing a beer can by putting it under his large belly.

"No of course it isn't me," he replied, feeling very embarrassed.

"But he looks just like you!" Tom replied. "Are you sure it isn't you?"

Graham clicked on one of the other videos the gentleman had uploaded and recoiled in shock as it was clearly in the category of gay fat fetish porn. It was very disturbing to see this doppelganger doing things he couldn't even have imagined in his wildest fantasies. He even had to think twice whether he at one point might have lost his memory for long enough to have enjoyed a career as an amateur gay porn star, they looked so similar.

"Of course it looks like me," Graham replied after having gathered his thoughts. "You searched for people that look like me, so obviously you'll see people looking like me as a result." He said this as much to reassure himself, as to answer Tom's question. It was pretty scary though how similar he looked to this man.

Melanie came back into the room and thankfully Tom had the decency to change the topic of the conversation.

When Graham went to bed that evening, he couldn't resist having another look at his doppelganger's videos. As much as he felt worried about people thinking that it was him in the videos, he was in admiration for this man having put them up publicly. The guy wasn't ashamed of his body and judging by the thousands of views his videos had had, there were clearly a lot of people who took pleasure from watching him. He eventually fell asleep while taking comfort in the fact that housewives with expensive pianos and his own mother were not the kind of people who would google the phrase "fat man crushing beer can with belly".

20

The next morning Graham woke up and lamented the fact that he had to put the scatter cushions back on the bed. The previous evening, Melanie had announced that people were coming to view the house, and could they please make sure that the bedrooms were presentable. He could hear Melanie pushing the hoover around downstairs.

He tried a few different ways of arranging the cushions but none looked very pleasing. If only he had taken a photo of the bed on his arrival so at least he had something to aim for. He even wished his doppelganger would walk through the door to help him out. Eventually, he settled for placing the cushions on their corners, like diamonds, forming two rows across the top of the bed. Not very original, but if this arrangement caused the house sale to fall through it probably wasn't meant to be.

He then went to check Dorene's bedroom which of course was immaculate. He remembered the hospital's request that he should bring some clothes with him and spotted her small cabin bag on the floor by the bed. He put it on the dressing table, opened it, and was presented with the familiar smell of his mum. He located a pair of knickers and felt slightly awkward touching them, followed by socks, trousers, and a blouse. Perhaps it would be easier just to bring the whole bag, he thought, and put the clothes back. As he closed it, an envelope slid out from the pocket on the inside of the top flap. It was yellow with age and addressed to someone called Dora Brown living in Oxford. The stamp was bold and beautiful and was from East Germany.

Graham pulled out a sheet with dense and old-fashioned handwriting. The date at the top said der 4. Juli 1959 and the letter began: Meine liebste Do, …

Graham didn't know any German and even if the handwriting was beautiful, it was pretty difficult to make out the words if you weren't familiar with the language.

"What's that?" said Tom when he entered the guest bedroom. He had a knack of knowing when there were secrets to be revealed and as usual had timed his appearance perfectly.

Graham jumped and quickly folded the page.

"No, let me see," Tom demanded and reached out for it. Graham reluctantly gave it to him, trying to remember if Tom had done any German at school.

"Is this a letter for Grandma?" he asked. Graham answered that the address said Dora on it and held up the envelope for Tom to see.

Tom got his phone out and held it up to the writing on the piece of paper. Graham had flashbacks from the previous day and worried about what would happen next.

"Crap, the handwriting is not clear enough, it only picks up a few words here and there. Look." Tom turned so that Graham could get a view of his phone. He saw a picture of the letter where there were little boxes of words in English popping up amongst the German, performing a merry dance on the screen while Tom was trying to hold the phone as still as possible. They both read as much as they could.

"Dearest Do,

When ... ... all ..... dead .... to kill ..... often .... without .... miss ,,, ... by your hand ..... meet .... to ..... good ..... in earnest ..... hide ..... hold .... heavy ... . don't tell .... instructions to follow .... burn .... messages ...... "

"Holy crap!" Tom exclaimed. "Grandma was a Nazi contract killer!"

Graham put the letter back in the lid pocket of the bag and zipped it up. "I'm sure she wasn't," he said to Tom and carried the bag with him downstairs. He kept thinking about the letter but couldn't quite make sense of it. He wasn't sure if there would be a suitable time to ask his mum about it. Maybe he should have it translated first.

Later that morning the hospital called and said Dorene was ready to be discharged. Graham asked Tom if he wanted to come along and Tom said OK. At the hospital, there seemed to be some confusion about Dorene's whereabouts and for a while Graham worried that she might have wandered off again. Eventually, they found she had been moved to a different ward late the previous evening and were given directions. When they found Dorene she was sitting on the edge of the bed in her hospital gown. On seeing Tom her face lit up and he walked up to her and gave her an awkward hug. Graham gave Dorene the bag and closed the curtains around the bed so she could put on some clothes.

A nurse appeared with a wheelchair and Tom seemed to enjoy pushing his Grandma through the maze of hospital corridors to the main entrance, where he waited while Graham got the car. Graham had strategically bought a pack of puppy training pads and had placed one on the passenger seat with a blanket on top, just in case.

When they returned to the house, the front door was wide open. Tom was the first to enter and was faced with the biggest mess he'd ever seen. Every drawer and cupboard had been emptied and the content thrown on the floor. The sofa cushions had been slashed and the stuffing pulled out. Melanie was nowhere to be seen.

21

Graham followed Tom into the house and was equally stunned.

"The people that came to view the house certainly took a very thorough look," Tom joked nervously. Dorene appeared behind Graham and looked at the mess in silence.

"I'd better phone the police," Graham said and then asked Tom to see if he and Dorene could wait at the neighbour's house.

While Graham was waiting for the police to arrive, he phoned Melanie but got straight to voicemail. He carefully looked in each room to make sure Melanie wasn't there. When looking in her bedroom, which had had the same treatment as the rest of the house, he spotted a pale blue note on the floor. It looked like a child had written it, but its content made Graham very worried. He didn't want to touch it in case it had fingerprints on it and instead returned downstairs. *Consequences indeed...*

When the police turned up they recognized him from a few days earlier and greeted him with a cheerful "We meet again!" which when coming from a police officer didn't feel particularly comforting. They took photos and dusted the place with fingerprint powder. He showed them the note and it was put in a plastic evidence bag. They asked him various questions and whether anything was missing but, as far as he could tell, Melanie herself was the only thing he could say with certainty was no longer there.

The police officers went next door to enquire whether someone might have seen or heard anything and was greeted by Helen, who looked very excited at the prospect of being questioned. She offered the officers coffee and homemade carrot cake as they joined Tom and Dorene in the kitchen. When Helen was asked if she had noticed anything, she nodded eagerly and started to describe a dark van that had pulled up outside Melanie's house. The officer who wasn't taking notes suddenly tugged at his colleague's arm and gestured for him to follow him into the hallway, where they had a quiet conversation. After a couple of minutes, they returned to the kitchen.

"Mrs Russell, could you come with us to the station please," one of the officers said, while the other put on plastic gloves and took a pad of light blue writing paper off the kitchen counter and slid it into a plastic evidence bag.

After the police officers escorted Helen out of the house, Tom and Dorene went back to see Graham. He'd already made a start on tidying up. There was now a path in the debris leading into the living room. The sofas looked like they had been on a drunken night out with the cushions lumpy and creased with bits of stuffing still sticking out here and there. Tom put the TV on and asked Dorene what she wanted to watch. She settled for Countdown and the two of them seem to enjoy watching it together. Graham had given Tom strict instructions not to let Dorene out of his sight, not even to go and make a cup of tea. This resulted in Graham tidying up the mess on his own, between bringing various refreshments into the living room. He didn't mind though. He tried Melanie's phone a number of times but it kept going straight to voicemail. The police had noted that her whereabouts weren't known, but were going to question Helen first and then make a decision on how to proceed.

They were just sitting down to eat some chilli and rice when Graham's phone rang. He was delighted to see Melanie as the caller id and answered "Melanie? Where   are   you?"

22

Melanie had just put a vase of autumn flowers from the garden on the dining table when the doorbell rang. It was only quarter to one, but maybe the viewers of the house were a bit earlier than arranged. She was expecting Mr and Mrs Patel, but the two gentlemen on the other side of the door certainly didn't fit the description, however open-minded she tried to be. She looked at the burly men wearing combat trousers and black leather jackets and when faced with the taller one's cold staring eyes, started feeling very nervous.

"Can I help you?" she asked tentatively.

"We hope so," the shorter man with a scar across his chin answered back with a distinctly Eastern European accent.

She tried to close the door, but one of them quickly put his foot in the way and within seconds they were both inside the house. She started running towards the patio doors but was knocked off her feet and pinned down so hard on the floor she couldn't even make a sound. Moments later she had her hands zipped-tied behind her back and a smelly rag stuffed inside her mouth. They lifted her up and put her on the sofa.

"Just 'cause your husband's dead doesn't mean you don't have to pay, little kitty," Scarface told her.

"Where's the money?"

Melanie wanted to ask what money they were referring to, but couldn't get a sound out of her mouth due to the rag.

The tall bearded one got a flick knife out of his pocket and held it to her throat as he pulled the cloth out of her mouth and repeated the question like he thought he had unplugged her ears.

"What money?" she asked, her voice now having a sprinkling of defiance in it.

"The fifty grand Stuart was supposed to pay us last week. Don't pretend you don't know about it," the short one told her cynically.

"I know absolutely nothing about that," Melanie said.

"Just tell us where the money is," the bearded one demanded, "or we'll just turn the house upside down until we find it."

When the short one realised that Melanie wasn't going to answer, he put the now damp cloth back in her mouth and stood up and looked around. The men nodded to each other and then started emptying every drawer and cupboard, throwing the contents on the floor. The bearded one went upstairs and, judging from the sounds, the first floor was receiving the same treatment. While the men were busying themselves wrecking the deceptively spacious and immaculately presented five-bedroom executive home, Melanie was trying to reach her mobile phone from her back pocket. Without drawing attention to herself, she finally managed to get her hands on it but soon cursed herself for having her lock screen use the facial recognition feature. She kept waiting for the opportunity to transfer the phone to her lap but each time she moved, the man nearest to her noticed and glared threateningly at her.

It didn't take the men long to trash the house and they reconvened in the living room trying to think of a plan B. They spoke between themselves in a foreign language. Melanie couldn't tell which, as all Eastern European languages sounded the same to her. After a few minutes deliberating, the tall one walked up to her and lifted her up by her arm and said "You're coming with us."

She dropped the phone which was picked up by the scarred man who then smiled smugly and slowly shook his head like she had been a naughty school girl. She was led out through the front door and quickly pushed into the back of the dark van onto hard plywood flooring that smelt of diesel. Moments later the van pulled out of the drive and she lost track of where she was going.

23

"No, this isn't Melanie. We've got Melanie," a heavily accented voice told Graham over the phone.

"What a relief! Is she ok?" Graham asked.

"No, what I meant was, we've kidnapped Melanie," came the reply, and Graham was lost for words.

"And we'll kill her if you go to the police," the deep voice continued.

"But we've already contacted the police," Graham blurted out. At this point, both Tom and Dorene had stopped talking and were listening carefully to try and figure out what was going on.

"Huh?" the kidnapper responded. "Well don't tell them we've contacted you and you'll still have a chance of seeing Melanie alive."

"But I'm sure the police are tracking her phone so they'll know you've called me," Graham said without thinking, which was met with silence before they terminated the call.

"Oh bollocks," Graham cursed to himself and looked at the phone. He then had to tell Tom and Dorene what had been said and apologised for having handled it so badly.

Within a few minutes, the phone rang again and once more the caller id said Melanie. Graham answered cautiously and decided to turn on the speaker so that Dorene and Tom could also hear and in that way share the burden of dealing with the kidnappers.

"Listen. You will tell the police that the calls you have received were from Melanie and that she's decided to take a short vacation and doesn't want to be disturbed. Or whatever, just make it up and make it sound believable. We don't want the police phoning us or we'll kill her, OK?"

"OK," Graham replied, determined not to say anything more than he had to.

"Is Melanie on holiday?" Dorene asked excitedly.

Graham closed his eyes and wished he'd not turned the speakerphone on.

"Who's that?" the kidnapper said angrily.

"My mother," Graham said with a sigh. "Sorry you're on loudspeaker."

"You idiot. Anyone else listening in?" came the immediate reply.

At this point, Tom quickly put his hand on Dorene's mouth and vigorously shook his head at Graham.

"No, no one else is here," Graham replied, trying to sound calm.

"To get Melanie back give us fifty grand tomorrow night at eight o'clock at the sharp bend of the quarry road where the farm track goes towards Black Lynn reservoir and if..." At this point Graham interrupted the kidnapper and explained that he wasn't local and had no idea where this was and did the man by any chance have a postcode or a what3words address for this place. The man sounded very annoyed but asked Graham to wait while he was talking in a strange language to someone else. After twenty seconds he was back on the phone saying "Here's your what3words: cycticercus, gynomonoecious, niggle."

Graham put on a confused face and looked at the others, but they both shrugged their shoulders indicating that they were as bewildered as he was.

"So you're saying the location is cyst, circus, gyno something or another and nigger?" Graham looked at the others for reassurance before continuing. "That sounds like four words to me and I'm pretty sure nigger shouldn't be one of them."

"No, I'll repeat, cycticercus, gynomonoecious, oh fuck it. I'll give you a different one. Here: firewall, nappies, October. Be there." And with that, the kidnapper hung up.

Tom had already entered the words into his phone and was now showing the location in google maps to Graham. It was a very remote place north of the city. Lots of options for both getting there and getting away as there was a multitude of little tracks weaving across the moorland.

"So, we know where to drop off the money. But where do we get the money from?" Graham asked more or less rhetorically.

"Also, you should have asked to speak to Melanie," Tom added. "You know, to prove they hadn't killed her already."

Graham nodded and contemplated phoning Melanie's phone again but decided not to as he felt he had annoyed the kidnappers enough already. For a while they sat in silence with nobody daring to say anything. They all pretty much had the same thoughts: Where would the money come from? And if they had the money, should they give it to the kidnappers?

The silence was broken when Graham's phone rang once again. This time it was the police. They enquired whether Melanie had been in touch and Graham cursed himself for not having spent the time preparing a plausible story in the few minutes he had had since the kidnappers had hung up. He waffled on about how she had phoned him and said that she needed to get away from the stress of the burglary and had decided to go somewhere peaceful and quiet for a few days and wouldn't be contactable.

"If you say so Mr Firth. It's just that we traced her phone to the Croftbank street twenty-six floor tower block in Springburn, which isn't exactly somewhere you'd want to go on holiday, if you see what I mean," the officer said slightly sarcastically.

"Ah, well Melanie finds the view from there very relaxing. Yes, thinking about it now, that's where she said she was when I spoke to her earlier. Visiting a friend. All makes sense." Graham wasn't good at lying and seeing Tom roll his eyes as he was speaking didn't make things any better.

The policeman told Graham that they had tried to phone Melanie but her phone was now switched off. If he spoke to Melanie again, he should tell her to call them as soon as possible and then they hung up.

Tom put the pan of chilli back on the stove while Dorene microwaved the rice. Graham remained seated at the table feeling like a popped balloon. They ate mostly in silence and when everyone's plate was empty Tom asked if it was ok if he went out. "I might be back later tonight, don't know yet."

"Sure that's fine. I'll call you if anything happens. But please be careful." Graham said abjectly.

Graham stacked the dishwasher helped by Dorene.

"I can't say I've enjoyed the last few days and I'm sure I can't remember everything that has happened, but I'm so grateful to be with you Graham," Dorene said while passing him the empty rice bowl.

"Thanks Mum. I don't feel I've handled things very well though," Graham replied.

"You have done nothing wrong. These Russians aren't going to kill Melanie until they have got the money. They'll just have to wait until we are ready," Dorene said like she had spent some time thinking about it.

"Russians? How can you be so sure they're Russians?" Graham said and stood up straight after putting the last plate in.

"They were speaking in Russian. Didn't you hear them?" Dorene said like it was obvious, before continuing, "Well I'm off to bed now. Am I trusted to sleep on my own or are you going to watch me now Tom's gone out?"

Graham was delighted that his mum seemed to be back to her old self and gave her a hug. "No, you'll be fine. See you in the morning," he said as he let go, watching Dorene leave the kitchen.

His thoughts went back to the letter he had found in Dorene's bag that same morning. Hopefully, he'd get a chance to ask her about it soon.

24

Helen was escorted into an interview room and was asked to sit down by a short chubby female officer who had introduced herself as inspector McMahan.

"I take it someone has explained to you that you are being interviewed under caution?" the officer asked after having turned on the recording equipment and sat down opposite Helen.

Helen nodded but was told to say yes verbally for the record.

"You have the right to legal advice, but I've been told you have declined this. Correct?" the inspector continued.

"Yes, that's correct," Helen said.

"We've found this letter at Eagles Nest Manor with content that could be interpreted as threats. Did you write this?" McMahan said and held up the clear plastic bag containing the blue sheet of paper found at Melanie's house.

Helen thought it was best to cooperate from the start, as it was all based on a misunderstanding anyway.

"Yes, I wrote it. You see, I was thinking Melanie was having an affair with my husband. I just wanted it to stop. I meant nothing by it. I've absolutely nothing to do with the break-in." Helen realized at this point the officer had no intention of interrupting her so she stopped talking.

"Yet, we have found your fingerprint in several places in the house," McMahan said and gestured to a pile of documents.

"Well, I have been in her house before today," Helen confessed.

"Could you please tell me when and what you were doing at Eagles Nest Manor prior to today?" the officer said with some disdain in her voice that really irritated Helen. Surely she should have some sympathy for her trying to keep her husband and not accepting some slut coming to steal him?

"Well, the first time was last Saturday night. Or maybe it was after midnight thinking about it. I heard someone scream and I found Stuart dead in the hot tub." Helen paused when she realized by the expression on the officer's face that Stuart's death was not something she had been aware of.

"By Stuart, you mean the same Stuart as you referred to in your letter?" she asked Helen.

"Yes exactly," Helen said.

"So *think of Stuart*, meant that you were threatening to kill Melanie?" the officer then added.

"No, no, you've got it all wrong. I wrote that to make her think she was insulting his memory by indulging in an affair so soon after his death. Not because I wanted her dead," Helen tried to clarify but wasn't sure it came across particularly well. She started to think that having a solicitor present might have been a good idea.

"Did you want Stuart dead?" came the next question. Helen felt more and more nervous.

"No of course not," she replied.

The officer picked up the phone and asked for somebody to join them in the room. Shortly thereafter there was a knock on the door and a mean-looking security guard entered.

"Sorry, I'm going to have to leave for a few minutes. Wait here and I'll be back soon," the female officer told Helen, who now was starting to feel a bit scared.

The security guard didn't look at all friendly and stared coldly at her like she was a criminal. Eventually, the chubby one came back with a male colleague with an Irish accent.

"I've decided to have my supervisor DCI O'Connor join us as we weren't aware of the death of Melanie's husband before now and I've just been told there have been some discoveries on the evidence front," McMahan said.

"Are you aware that Melanie is missing?" DCI O'Connor asked Helen in a gentle voice that Helen immediately took to. Perhaps he would understand what she was trying to explain and not try and twist everything like the other one, Helen thought.

"No," she replied while trying to remember the last time she saw Melanie.

"We believe that the person who broke into her house might have something to do with her disappearance," the Chief Inspector informed her. Helen nodded slowly.

"Perhaps you could explain what her shoes were doing in your car?" O'Connor added, dashing Helen's hopes that she would be allowed home anytime soon.

25

Tom wasn't sure he wanted to see Jack, but if someone knew the Springburn area it was him. His family had lived there until he was twelve, before moving to the cheaper end of Bearsden in the hope that their offspring's aspirations might improve. As the parents soon found out, the children's ties to their friends on the estate had been difficult to break. The friendships formed while running from druggies that wanted to steal your school dinner money tended to run deep. Instead of being one of the best performing students in his class Jack found himself near the bottom of his new class and struggled to make new friends. Tom was one of the few Bearsden friends he had made and that was only because Tom had also been a newcomer.

Tom cycled over on Josie's bike, which he still hadn't returned. When he pulled up outside Jack's house he could see him wrestling Josh in the front room. Tom stood outside in the semi-darkness and watched the two brothers as they pulled and bent each other in a violent but still affectionate way. After a while, Jack seemed to get the upper hand and pinned Josh down in an armchair while managing to pull the stretchy sleeves of his jumper around the back of the chair and secure them with a big knot. Josh was trapped and started to laugh. It seemed to Tom that it was a good moment to enter.

Jack looked delighted to see Tom.

"Awricht, ye bawbag, sorry for earlier. It was the mushies you know. Come in." Jack greeted Tom with the assumption that all was forgiven. Apology out of the way, Tom could start telling Jack what had happened to Melanie.

"Ah've got mates fae Croftbank. They're not gangsters but they mibbe know who did this. Get oan the bike and we'll boost ower there and see," Jack said, grabbed a coat and headed for the door.

"What about Josh?" Tom asked.

"No, betta leave him outta this," Jack replied before realizing that Tom was referring to him being tied up in the living room.

Jack and Tom made their way to Springburn and Tom could tell this was a route Jack knew very well. He struggled to keep up as Jack sped through red lights and jumped up curbs to take shortcuts by using the pavement. In less than half an hour they were staring up at the tall apartment block on Croftbank Street.

"What do we do now?" Tom asked, feeling slightly nervous being in Springburn after dark.

"Ye wait here. We cannae leave the bikes or they'll be nicked faster than a swallow on speed. Ah'm gonnae to ask around," Jack said and disappeared through the main entrance leaving Tom on his own holding the two bikes.

Tom felt scared and very middle class. He was convinced people were giving him funny looks as they walked past. He tried to adopt a mean facial expression by pretending he'd just nicked the bikes he was holding and was getting into the role when an unhealthy looking man walked past and shouted "Aye, laddie! How much for the bikes?" Thankfully the man quickly walked away when a couple of police cars pulled up.

Tom softened his stance to not draw attention to himself, but the officers didn't even glance his way before entering the Croftbank Street building. Tom occasionally shared glances with the officer that was left behind to guard the vehicles, feeling both reassured and nervous at the same time. Tom waited for what seemed like forever without the police officers or Jack reappearing. It was now dark and he was shivering. Eventually, the police officers returned, got back in their vehicles and drove off. He couldn't tell whether their visit had anything to do with Melanie possibly being captive in the building.

Finally, Jack came back with his usual wide grin, giving Tom some hope of good news.

"And?" Tom said and handed him his bike.

"Nah, nothin," he replied. "No one ah spoke to has seen a rich lass coming or leaving this place. Not even nosy Pete, and he'd know. Sorry," Jack said and then added "Fancy some fried chicken? There's a great place around the corner."

Tom said yes and followed Jack. He had no idea what was going to happen now. At least he'd tried his best by following the only lead he had had. Short of robbing a bank, he couldn't see what else he could do to help.

26

Seeing the ripped-up scatter cushions discarded around the bedroom had given Graham a brief moment of joy. He had taken great pleasure in putting them and their cheap wadding into a bin bag before going to bed. Unfortunately, he had then spent most of the night tossing and turning, unable to switch off. Hearing Tom return home gave him only temporary relief. As soon as he started to drift off some part of his brain injected another burst of adrenaline and he'd become wide awake again.

In the morning he was dreaming that he was back in his old bedroom as a child and it was the school summer holidays. He could hear his mum playing Elvira Madigan on the piano. Everything was simple and carefree apart from that Stuart was knocking annoyingly on the headboard and he wished he would stop. He was pulled out of his peaceful dream, knock by knock, when he heard Tom on the other side of the door calling "Graham, are you awake?"

He opened his eyes and expected the piano music to stop but it didn't. It continued and it was beautiful.

"I'll be down in a minute," he told Tom.

He got up and felt surprisingly cheerful as he entered the living room, seeing his mother at the piano. Her body movements, as her fingers floated over the keys, were like a ballet dancer who had lost the use of her legs. It was a vision that enhanced the sounds coming from the piano. Tom joined him and they watched in silence. But there was something not quite right. There was a dullness to the notes, particularly higher up in the register, which Graham didn't recognize from his childhood. Perhaps the piano had been damaged when it was moved or by the thugs that had almost taken the whole house apart. He went to the kitchen and made a cup of coffee while Tom poured himself a pint of orange juice and put the empty juice carton back in the fridge. Graham couldn't bring himself to complain.

"What are we going to do?" Tom asked Graham.

"I don't know," Graham replied. "I've been thinking about it all night. Do you happen to know if Melanie has any relatives that might help?"

Tom shook his head. "No, her parents are both dead. Her sister lives in Australia and they haven't spoken for 20 years I think."

"Rich and friendly ex-husband?" Graham suggested.

"No," Tom replied, "more like the opposite. Apparently he was a right tosser."

"Then maybe our only option is getting the police involved," Graham said with a sigh.

He took his coffee and went back to the living room where Dorene had stopped playing and was now looking through the sheet music stored inside the compartment of the piano stool. Clearly, the gangsters weren't familiar with piano stools as its content hadn't been spread onto the floor in their search for whatever they had been looking for.

He put his cup down on the coffee table and asked Dorene if she'd mind him taking a look at the piano to see what was causing the slight dullness he had noticed earlier.

He flipped the front top board over and took a look at the rows of dampers, but couldn't see anything out of the ordinary. He continued by releasing the catches on either side and removed the upper front board to expose the mechanisms, which looked shiny and complicated to an untrained eye. He pressed a few keys in the higher register and observed the movements carefully. Everything looked normal but he could clearly hear the difference in tone now and the cause must be located lower down. He then flipped the metal spring to take off the lower front board and immediately spotted that something wasn't right. There were square bundles wrapped in plastic taped to every accessible surface inside the piano, including the back of the board he had just removed.

"What's this, mum?" he asked, as he pulled one of the bundles off the sidewall.

Dorene came closer and watched Graham unwrap a half an inch thick bundle of twenty-pound notes.

"It looks like money to me," she said cautiously, wondering if it was a trick question.

"Yes, but do you know what it's doing here?" Graham added for clarification.

"No idea. I don't think I put it in there," she replied with an amount of uncertainty in her voice.

They pulled out bundle after bundle and unwrapped a

few to check that they all contained money. There must have been at least fifty thousand pounds.

Tom entered the living room carrying a bowl of cereal. On seeing the money he went:

"Whoa! Where did you get that?"

"It was in there," Dorene said and pointed at the piano.

"Do we have to give it to the kidnappers?" Tom asked after a few seconds, his concern for Melanie being somewhat downgraded when presented with so much money. "After all Graham, it is your money," he then added, clearly out of politeness.

"No, I'm sure it isn't," Graham replied.

"But my Dad left you the piano, didn't he?" Tom added with a pragmatic tone.

"What do you mean?" Dorene chipped in. "It is my piano. Always has been."

Graham could sense that things were getting complicated and said in a firm voice that surprised both Tom and Dorene "Yes mum, the piano is yours, but the money was most likely put there by Stuart or Melanie so it isn't for us to keep. To be honest, it's probably what the kidnappers were after and couldn't find, so that's why they took Melanie instead. And I'm pretty sure Stuart wasn't supposed to have this money or it would have been in the bank." Graham paused for a moment before adding "At least now we'll be able to do the exchange after all."

Dorene agreed but Graham noticed that Tom looked disappointed.

The three of them sat there looking at the pile of money when there was a knock on the front door. Tom got up and looked out through the living room window and announced "Shit, the police are here."

27

Graham let the police in after having helped Tom and Dorene put the money back inside the piano as quickly as possible. There were two young male officers that Graham didn't recognize and they apologised for calling in unannounced. They had been doing a search next door and would he mind if they asked him some questions.

Graham brought them into the dining area and offered them coffee which they politely declined.

"Have you heard from Melanie?" PC Barley, the thin blond officer asked. To which Graham gave an honest no and then added "I'm actually getting a bit worried. What the police said yesterday about her being in Springburn. Do you think she has been abducted?" Graham was grateful for the opportunity to look less suspicious. Hopefully, tomorrow all this would be history.

"We have evidence to suggest Mrs Russell from nextdoor has had some involvement with the burglary and also with Melanie's disappearance. How well do you know Mrs Russell?" the officer asked Graham.

"Not at all. She popped over for a coffee on Tuesday morning but didn't stay more than ten minutes. She certainly didn't seem keen on Melanie," Graham added. Not because he meant Helen any harm but it suited

Graham to draw attention away from money laundering eastern European gangsters at this point in time. Once Melanie was back, any misunderstandings could quickly be cleared up.

"Were you here between Saturday and Sunday, the night Stuart Firth died?" PC Barley asked and Graham shook his head.

"No, I came up with Dorene, my mum, on Monday afternoon. We live down Cheshire way," he explained.

"Right," the officer said, "Do you mind if I take a look in the garden where he died?"

"Please, go ahead," Graham said and opened the patio doors.

The other officer went into the living room where Tom and Dorene were watching TV trying to look relaxed. They were asked similar questions but again were unable to shed much light on Helen's motive or what had happened the previous weekend.

As soon as the police officers had left, Tom got his phone out from his back pocket. He had felt it vibrate on and off during the questioning but thankfully nobody else had noticed. The phone showed eight missed calls from Jack so Tom quickly made his way up to his bedroom.

"Jack, what did you want?" Tom said when Jack answered.

"Got news ye eejit. Big Dom just phoned me. He knows who's got Melanie. It's the Russians." Jack said triumphantly.

"Is that a good thing or not?" Tom asked.

"Not really. They aren't very nice and have been

sniffing around trying to get into stuff, if ye know what I mean. Upset some of the locals. And some of the big guys too. Bad news is, nobody knows where they've gone. They're not at Croftbank anymore."

"That's ok, we've found some money so we can get Melanie back anyway," Tom announced.

"You found fifty grand? What, like at the back of the sofa or summat?" Jack asked incredulously.

"Something like that," Tom replied.

Jack went quiet for a long time and in the end Tom asked him if he was still on the line.

To which Jack replied "Tom, get ower 'ere quick. I've got an idea."

28

Graham was happy that Tom had decided to go out and was now sitting with Dorene at the dining table with a big pile of cash in front of him. To have had Tom there, drooling over the money and talking non-stop, would have made it a lot harder to count it all.

After checking it twice they were fairly certain that they had £51 560 pounds at their disposal. They wrapped up fifty grand in thousand-pound bundles using rubber bands and put the bundles in a large black handbag which was hanging under some coats in the hallway.

Graham went to the kitchen and returned carrying cups of coffee which he put down on the dining table. It seemed like this might be a good opportunity to ask about Dora.

"I found a letter in your bag yesterday before getting you from the hospital," Graham said and looked at Dorene, who was scraping the bottom of the sugar jar with a teaspoon.

"What letter?" she asked Graham while stirring her coffee vigorously.

"It was addressed to Dora Brown," Graham added, worried that he might be upsetting his mother.

"Ah, I'd forgotten that was in there," she answered and then remained silent for what seemed like forever to

Graham.

She finally broke the silence by saying "Well, it was a very long time ago now. What do you want to know?"

Her reluctance to volunteer any information made Graham think she would rather not talk about it. However, if he didn't say anything now, there would probably never be a better moment.

"Is the letter for you?" he finally asked.

"Yes, my name before I married your father was Brown. And as you probably saw, the letter was from before I got married," Dorene answered rather defensively.

"It's in German isn't it?" Graham asked cautiously.

"Yes, it was sent from someone in East Germany who I was quite close to," Dorene said and Graham noticed how sad Dorene looked even though she wouldn't make eye contact with him while she was speaking.

"How come you also know Russian?" Graham asked. He felt guilty that his curiosity was greater than his misgivings about making his mum sad.

"Everyone in East Germany had to learn Russian. It was taught the moment you started school," Dorene answered and then realized Graham was staring at her with a surprised look on his face. "I never told you did I," she added. "I was born in Berlin and moved to England in 1959," she said and sighed. "Perhaps I should have told you sooner."

"Did you escape across the wall?" Graham asked.

Dorene gave Graham a look of disbelief.

"It wasn't even built then and do you really think the

Stasi would send love letters to someone who had climbed over the Berlin wall? " she said with some incredulity. She then realised that Graham had not been aware who the sender of the letter was and again wished she had kept her mouth shut.

"Well, I suppose I'll need to tell you the rest now. I wasn't going to, you know. Some things are best left, but if you insist," she said and looked Graham straight in the eye.

Graham first didn't realize that Dorene wanted an answer but said "Yes please" when he realized she wasn't going to continue without his consent.

"My parents weren't from Birmingham and they weren't killed in a car crash, as you were told when you were little. They were still in East Germany until they died in the late 1980s," Dorene said before taking a short pause and sipping her coffee. "I'm ashamed to say they both worked for the Stasi. Both were committed communists, convinced that what they were doing was for the good of the country. I thought so too. We were pretty well off compared to the others. You were if you were part of the Stasi because they knew how to look after you," Dorene said and then looked straight ahead for a long time, seemingly lost in distant memories. Graham didn't want to speak for fear of saying the wrong thing and waited patiently for Dorene to continue. He found it hard to believe that less than a week ago the most exciting thing that had happened to him was having a power cut in a cinema and now he was dealing with a dead brother, kidnappers, large sums of suspicious money, and a mother who for all he knew had been a Stasi contract killer.

"Obviously my parents signed me up with the Free German Youth as the earlier they could brainwash you the better. I used to get pocket money for telling my parents what the other children in my class said and sometimes those children just disappeared, never to be seen again. I still feel bad about it now." Dorene looked up at Graham. "Isn't it funny that I can't remember what I had for breakfast, but I remember the friends I never saw again? I can still picture their faces in front of me." Dorene got up and left the room and Graham remained seated. He considered getting up to make sure Dorene was ok, but resisted as he suspected she needed a moment to herself. He heard the downstairs loo being flushed and he was relieved when Dorene came back to the dining table.

"And how did you end up here?" Graham asked to force Dorene to continue her story. It took Dorene a few seconds to grasp what he meant before she continued.

"I've always been good at languages and my parents made me learn both Russian and English fluently. For some reason, my English was particularly good and in my late teens I was told I could serve our country by spying on the enemy. To a seventeen-year-old, it sounded like an adventure, as you can imagine. So I was sent to a military school for training." Dorene noticed the fear on Graham's face when she said this and reassured him that the training was in cryptography and English and not in how to kill people, although she had been taught how to use a gun. She told Graham how she had been given a new identity, Dora Brown, with a made-up history. If anyone asked she had to pretend that she had been born in Austria to English parents. Her father had supposedly been a psychologist with a private practice. She explained how she had been sent to England via Vienna to study art history in Oxford with a bag full of fake introductory letters to make sure she could gain entry into the inner circles of the future leaders of Britain. There had been one snag however. Three months before leaving as a fresh-faced nineteen-year-old she had fallen in love with Axel, a fellow student at the military school. Feelings had been overwhelming, as they always are at that age, and she had not wanted to leave for Britain anymore. The state was not going to squander years of planning and investment and had threatened to send Dorene to a labour camp if she didn't comply and also punish her parents. It was with despair and disgust towards her country she finally left, leaving behind the love of her life, but taking away the embryo that had embedded itself into her womb.

When she arrived in England she felt a sense of newly won freedom, a feeling that she had never had before. This, combined with the sudden grudge she bore against her country made her delay contacting her handler. Let them sweat for a bit she'd thought while she settled in at the local halls of residence at the college where she was studying. She was enjoying the course and felt strangely comfortable with her new identity even though she missed Axel terribly.

A month went by and she realized she was pregnant. It could have been her ticket home, as she now was pretty useless as a spy, but there was no guarantee that there wouldn't be repercussions if she returned. And anyway, she suspected that by the time she'd reached East Germany, Axel would also have been posted somewhere. In the same way as she hadn't been allowed to tell him about her new identity, they had kept his new identity secret to avoid compromising the security of their surveillance operations.

She decided to keep studying for as long as she could get away with it. There was nothing that the Stasi could do to her now without also compromising itself and its espionage network. As long as she hadn't made contact she was safe. A month later the letter had arrived from Axel. She had cried for hours as it was the first time in over two months she had heard from him. He was saying all the lovely things she wanted to hear. How he would rather be dead than to live without her because he missed her so. How he could try and arrange for her to return to East Germany. She quickly realized that he had been given her address by Stasi and told exactly what to write to try and get her back, now they had realized she wasn't going to obey their instructions. The last thing they wanted was a loose cannon potentially turning on them and joining the enemy ranks. This made her cry even more. She had wanted to reply but realised that it wasn't likely Axel would even be allowed to read her reply. She tried her best to forget him, but every now again re-read the letter and wondered what would have happened had she written back.

Graham listened attentively and started feeling like he was in a parallel world where everything he thought he knew turned out to be wrong and nothing ever stopped spinning long enough for him to get a grasp of the situation.

"So what did you do?" he asked Dorene. He probably had been able to guess the last bit, but he wanted to hear her say it. To stop himself from ever doubting.

"Well, I knew I had to leave the college when my bump started to show, and with no means of supporting myself I did what any girl would have done." Dorene stopped and looked with sad eyes at Graham.

"And that was?" Graham asked.

"Well, I met your dad. He seemed nice. He was just about to finish his PhD and was teaching undergraduates. He wasn't what you'd call handsome but he was a very nice man and we were very happy." Dorene noticed a funny look on Graham's face and added "No, we really were happy and I loved him very much."

Graham continued to stare at her and she suddenly realized why. "Sorry, you are right. He wasn't your dad, but he never said anything about it and I didn't say anything either so we kind of just forgot about it. It happened a lot in those days. It was just the easiest way. I always thought of him as your dad."

"Did Axel ever find out?" Graham enquired, strangely relieved that what he had suspected from the moment he had seen the letter had now been said.

"No, I never went back or contacted him. Too dangerous. I have no idea what happened to him although I did think about looking for him after your dad died. But it didn't seem fair after all these years. We only knew each other for a few months."

"What was his surname?" Graham asked to which Dorene reluctantly answered Zoransky.

Graham remained seated, deep in thoughts, when Dorene announced that she felt tired and was going for a lie-down.

29

When Tom arrived at Jack's house there were tools and bikes scattered on the front lawn. Josh was using gaffer tape to repair a bright orange bicycle trailer, while Jack was trying to attach a bracket to the chainstay of his blue Apollo bike. There was a lot of swearing going on.

"Awricht! Glad ye got 'ere, thought ye weren't comin!" Jack shouted when he spotted Tom. Tom wasn't sure how to react as he thought he'd wasted no time in getting there.

"Wannae hear my plan then?" Jack continued and gave Tom a devious-looking smile.

"OK," Tom replied. He had felt a little nervous walking over, and seeing that even Josh was involved in whatever Jack had planned hadn't helped. Jack often started things that got out of hand.

"The handover's still happening, isnae it?" Jack asked Tom, who nodded. "At the place ye said?" Jack continued.

"Yeah, I think so," Tom answered.

"Stoatin'! We need some signs put up. Ah tell ye the rest later," Jack said and handed Tom a screwdriver.

They set to attaching the trailer to the bike and Jack rode it around the block to make sure it wouldn't come off. The three of them were soon cycling towards an area north of the city, which according to the council website was being resurfaced the following morning. You could say a lot about Jack, but he certainly was resourceful and a true entrepreneur. Tom often wished he was as brave. Just a shame that so many of Jack's ideas weren't strictly legal.

After a bit of hunting, they had filled the trailer with four road closed signs and five yellow diversion signs, including their stands. The trailer creaked under the strain as they cycled toward the handover location on the moorland hills about four miles away. They eventually left the main road and continued up a steep badly tarmacked road. Thankfully they were able to get rid of a couple of the signs early, by positioning them at junctions along the way, making it slightly easier for Jack to pedal. Tom had at this point figured out that Jack's plan involved making sure that the kidnappers were forced to come back the same way they had come, by blocking off any alternative routes. The road was in pretty poor condition with large potholes and eroded edges so it wasn't far-fetched that it was due some road repairs.

As they were putting up a sign close to the top of the hill, a car overtook them and pulled into a layby. Tom, Josh, and particularly Jack, were hot and red-faced from the exhaustion of cycling up the hill when a thin grey man wearing gaiters and holding a pair of telescopic walking poles got out of the car. Judging by the look on the older man's face, he wasn't about to give them praise for their cycling stamina. Jack realised this before anyone else and shouted a loud "Guid day, sir!" before the man had opened his mouth.

"Ye'll be OK parking there. Wir no starting the resurfacing until tomorrow," Jack said in a friendly and informative way to the man who now was forced to re-evaluate the situation. Tom was amazed by how professional Jack sounded and nodded toward the walker to back up Jack's statement.

"Ye'd think the council could think of a betta way than this to be carbon neutral, wouldn't ye?" Jack added and laughed as they all cycled past the man who hadn't managed to utter a single word.

At the junction, where the handover was due to happen that evening, they positioned the last two road closed signs and used the arrows to send the traffic back to where it had come from.

"That should do it," Jack said. "Just need tae call into Poundland and pick up a few bits n' bobs and then we're done."

They turned their bike around and coasted down towards Glasgow, the kiddie trailer bouncing left and right behind Jack's bike.

30

Melanie woke up and tried to stretch her legs but they hit a hard concrete surface. She pushed hard and managed to move her body forwards a few inches on the rough floor. Every bone in her body ached and she felt very cold. At least the floor of the van had provided some insulation and hadn't been drafty. She almost regretted having used her forehead to bang against the side panel of the van after she had heard the men leave the vehicle. Instead of drawing attention from potential rescuers, the kidnappers had returned to the van and driven her somewhere else.

She had no idea where she was as she still had the cloth bag over her head, but guessed she had been put in a garage or lockup of sorts. It smelt damp and mouldy and was too quiet for comfort. She had been sitting up for as long as possible but eventually the strain on her shoulders and arms, that were still secured firmly behind her back, had become too much. She had managed to find a less uncomfortable position lying down, curled up to save whatever warmth she could generate from her own body. Eventually, she had fallen asleep.

She tried to guess how long she had been in the kidnappers' hands and judging by how full her bladder was it must be at least eight hours or more. It was becoming increasingly difficult to control and she pulled up her legs as close to her body as she could to try and alleviate the pressure. She didn't think there was anyone else there with her but tried to call out just in case. The kidnappers had replaced the rag with a strip of tape, so the only sound that came out of her mouth was a dull moan that was unlikely to attract anyone's attention.

In the end, she couldn't hold it in anymore and let it go. The warmth was more pleasant than she had anticipated and she savoured every second of it. She felt similar to the occasions when she had been very drunk and she had let go of everything beyond her control and entered a fatalistic and nearly catatonic state where just being was enough. The only thing she had been able to control at this point had been her bladder and now she had let go of that, freeing herself from any remaining responsibilities. There was nothing left that she could do or change regarding her situation and it made her feel strangely calm. Everything had truly gone pear-shaped now and for the first time in her life, she felt that she didn't care about what would happen next.

She wished she had had this strength twenty years ago, just after she had qualified as a dentist. A week into her first job, she had accidentally dropped a dental cotton roll down a female patient's windpipe. It was the worst minute of her life as she was trying to retrieve it while the lady was trying to get out of the chair. Eventually, the patient had fought her off, sat up, and coughed the white roll across the treatment room. She had then torn her paper bib off and thrown her safety glasses at Melanie and had stormed out to the reception, while shouting that she nearly had been killed. The experience had lodged itself in Melanie's brain, playing itself over and over until Melanie had started having panic attacks when merely being near the dental practice. She had thrown five years of university education away and instead had completed a couple of college courses to become a nail technician and a colon hydrotherapist, neither involving accidentally choking people to death. It had always pained her that she had let one bad experience ruin her career. Had she stuck with it, she might not have been a broke, homeless, and kidnapped widow. One that had just weed her own pants and enjoyed it. Soon the wet denim jeans cooled down and even that pleasure was gone.

Suddenly aluminium panels were clattering and a gust of fresh air made Melanie's jeans feel even colder than before. There was no difference in the light that she could detect through the cloth bag so she guessed that it was dark outside. She heard the shutters close again and saw flashes of light that must be from a flashlight. A pair of strong arms lifted her into a sitting position and the bag was pulled off her head. The same two men that had taken her were both crouching down looking at her with a peculiar mix of disgust and desire.

Scarface put his finger up to his lips to signal to her to be quiet, while his companion pulled the tape off her mouth and put a bottle of water against her lips. She drank too quickly and ended up coughing violently while the man tried to cover her mouth with his hand to shut her up. It took a couple of minutes before she was able to breathe normally again.

"Your brother-in-law is an idiot," Scarface told her.

"Has he got money?"

"I don't know," Melanie started. "I don't think so. Not much anyway."

"Anyone else that might be able to pay the money? Any friends or rich relatives?" the scarred man asked, his breath smelling of boiled cabbage and alcohol.

"No, my parents are dead and my sister hates me," Melanie confessed sadly.

"We'll give him a chance to get the cash and see what happens. But I'm not holding my breath."

Although Melanie hoped that he would.

They let her eat a banana by shoving it into her mouth bit by bit and then spread out a thin mattress and a flaccid pillow on the floor. She shuffled her bottom onto it and laid down after a fresh piece of tape had been put over her mouth. A blanket that smelt of cat piss was put over her body, but she was still grateful.

She heard the clattering of the shutters as the two men left.

"Well, I'm not at rock bottom anymore," she thought, as she was no longer hungry or cold.

31

Graham made himself another cup of coffee and sat down at the kitchen table. His curiosity got the better of him and he googled Alex Zoransky. Judging from the results there were a few of them and he quickly ruled out an American basketball player in his 20s, a lesbian Australian dramatist, and a Polish poet from the late 1800s. He selected the image tab hoping to more easily find a plausible match and scrolled down until he spotted a photo of two rather stout gentlemen smiling and shaking hands in front of the camera. The site mentioned a deal between a large Russian gas company and an Austrian cooperation that had taken place in 2005. Graham looked closely at the gentleman on the right and maybe there were some similarities between himself and this man. It was hard to tell. He read the article and found out that Zoransky possibly lived in St Petersburg, not exactly former East Germany but not a million miles away. If he had stayed in the Stasi, it is likely he would have moved to Russia as a means of avoiding prosecution and humiliation after the wall fell.

Graham then searched for Zoransky and St Petersburg and was rewarded with several photos of the same gentleman and one with him together with two children, a boy and a girl that looked like it was taken in the late 1970s. Graham shuddered as he remembered the photo in Dorene's room of him and Stuart. The boy in the photo looked just like he had at that age. The similarities were spooky. He was a chunky boy, not quite as chunky as Graham had been at that age, but not far off. He thought back to the video of the man with the beer can. He found one of the clips and the username of the account said "R FitZ". Graham set about watching the videos to find clues to where the man was from. It wasn't easy only having the small screen of his phone available. He scrutinized every detail in the videos, from the tattoos of the many naked bodies on display, to the style of electrical sockets that you could sometimes spot. It was in the ninth video he finally struck lucky, a poster above the bed had Cyrillic script and pictured the famous gay icon Vladimir Putin. Graham wasn't sure whether this proved anything, but the urge to find out more was overwhelming. Perhaps the fact that he had just lost one brother made him even keener to find a new one. He jumped when suddenly the doorbell rang.

Graham opened the door to see Mike. As Graham greeted him, the phone he was holding in his hand started emitting loud groaning noises. He desperately tried to turn off the video while apologising to Mike.

"Don't worry about it," Mike said sympathetically. Graham wanted to explain, but realised that Mike would never believe him if he told him the truth and decided to carry on as if it hadn't happened. They sat down in the dining area and Graham couldn't help thinking that the man in front of him looked much smaller and older than when he'd met him at the hospital.

"I've come to apologise and explain," Mike started.

"I want to begin by saying how sorry I am."

Graham wasn't quite sure what Mike meant and then remembered that it was only last night Helen had been arrested by the police suspected of having abducted his sister-in-law. "Don't worry, I'm sure..." Graham said but was interrupted by Mike.

"You see, it isn't the first time she's done this. She struggles with her mental health and gets these ideas. Especially when it comes to neighbours or nurses. She can't do anything about the nurses of course, but we've moved seven times in the last twelve years. I've even tried to make sure we move somewhere where the neighbours are really old to avoid her getting suspicious, but invariably a young couple moves in somewhere close by. She's even had a couple of restraining orders put on her in the past. But this is in a different league altogether. I just don't know what to think." Mike put his head in his hands as he rested his elbows on the dining table.

Graham wasn't sure what to think either. He had assumed the kidnappers were connected to Stuart's dodgy land dealings based on what Melanie had told him the other night and the fact that jealous spouses were probably more interested in revenge than large sums of cash. He'd almost forgotten about Helen and her note.

"Anyway, I just wanted to say how sorry I am and that Melanie, god forbid something has happened to her, shouldn't feel that she needs to sell the house. I suspect we'll be moving again soon," Mike said.

"Ah," Graham replied, "you shouldn't worry about

the for-sale signs as Melanie was putting the house on the market anyway. I doubt that it has anything to do with Helen's letter. Also, I wouldn't be surprised if she'll just turn up soon." Graham stopped there as he felt that if he kept talking he would end up telling Mike everything and jeopardising the handover later that night.

"That's very kind of you to say," Mike said and stood up. He then enquired about how Dorene was doing and finished by offering to help Graham in any way he could.

Just after Mike left, Dorene came downstairs. Graham announced he was going to start cooking dinner early so that there was no rush before they were due to go to the handover location.

"Ooo, a trip out!" Dorene exclaimed. "Will Stuart and Melanie be joining us?"

32

Tom followed Jack home. It was clear that his friend had the whole thing organised but was reluctant to share his plans with him. Tom was worried but felt he had no choice other than to go along with it. This mission, whatever it was, was going to happen regardless if Tom came along or not.

Jack asked if Tom was hungry but didn't wait for an answer before leaving the living room. The rest of the house looked tidy in comparison to the kitchen, which genuinely looked like a bomb had hit it. There were dirty pans and plates on every surface and the bin was overflowing with empty pizza boxes. In many ways, it resembled Melanie's kitchen from the day before, with the difference being that everything would need to be washed before being returned to the cupboards and drawers.

"Are your parents not here?" Tom asked as he looked at the mess, the second such mess he's seen in twenty-four hours.

"Nah, they're on holiday. How jammy am I!" Jack replied and grinned like he had won the jackpot.

"When are they coming back?" Tom asked as there was no way he'd risk being present when Mr and Mrs Simmonds returned.

"Tomorrow, I think," Jack replied as he stuck his

head in the fridge. He got out a jar of mayo and then went to a cupboard where he found a tin of tuna and a tin of sweetcorn. A bag of penne pasta was fished out of a plastic grocery bag on the kitchen floor. Tom, feeling concerned about the general hygiene standards, started washing up a large pan which he then filled with water and handed to Jack.

Just as the pasta was cooked, Josie walked into the kitchen. Tom and Josie nodded to each other and there was a moment of awkward silence while they deliberated whether to mention the phone thing. In the end, Jack broke the silence and asked Josie if she wanted some dinner.

"Will ye wash some plates, Tom? No clean ones left," Jack said and opened the tins and emptied the tuna and sweetcorn into the pan of drained pasta.

Josie called Josh and soon the four of them were eating in the living room, plates on knees, watching the news on the TV.

"C'mon then, let's get ready," Jack announced when they had all finished eating and spent an adequate amount of time digesting the starchy food.

To Tom's surprise, Josie also got up and started packing a small backpack with a torch, gloves, and a hat.

"Is she coming too?" Tom asked Jack quietly.

"Sure, she's the key element!" replied Jack and again gave Tom a fiendish smile. "Have ye got a torch Dickhead?" he continued.

Tom shook his head.

"No worries. Picked up a spare from Poundland for

155

ye," Jack said and handed Tom a cheap head torch. Jack proceeded to pack a small water pistol, a pair of pliers, and a mosquito head net into a dark blue backpack. Tom felt under-equipped. He hadn't even thought of bringing a pair of gloves. It looked like it was going to be a cold evening now the sun had set.

Josh appeared from his room with his face all covered in camo paint.

"FFS Josh what ye playing at, we're no in the IRA, we'll get chinned by the polis soon as we step oot the door rigged oot like that," Jack told Josh who looked disappointed and ready to abandon the whole thing.

"Ok then, as ye'll be in the kiddie trailer it doesn't really matter," Jack continued, worried about upsetting Josh.

"Why is Josh going to be in the trailer?" Tom asked Jack.

"Because ye're taking his bike this time. Unless ye want to go in the trailer?" Jack added.

Tom said no and Jack handed him the backpack and said "Ye take this, I'll have enough weight dragging Josh behind me."

They all went outside and Josh managed to adopt what looked like a very advanced yoga position that made him small enough to fit in the trailer. It didn't look very comfortable. Tom felt guilty about not having brought his bike along but was impressed to see that someone had already put the saddle up on Josh's bike to a more suitable height. Tom was a good six inches taller than Josh. Perhaps Jack had all this under control after all.

The four of them made their way back to the high moorland roads above Glasgow. It was getting darker but the sky was still light enough to avoid using lights. When they had reached the tiny road that took them up the hill to the handover location, Jack pulled over.

"You two, plank yer arse here. No need for ye to cycle all the way up. Me and Josh'll fire up and then I'll come back and let ye know what we're doin'. Tam, geez the bike, yer arse I'm kerting this nugget up on ma ain," Jack said and laughed as Josh tried to extract himself from the trailer.

Soon Jack and Josh were heading up the hill. The saddle was set far too high for Josh, forcing him to pedal standing up. It was seven o'clock and nearly dark and an hour until the kidnappers would arrive.

33

Graham spent a long time over dinner explaining to Dorene what they were about to do. Initially, she had looked at him as if he was pulling her leg, but slowly she started to remember what was going on. Or at least pretended to. Graham started to regret not having got the police involved.

According to his phone, it would take twenty minutes to drive to the agreed location, but since Graham was unfamiliar with the area and it was dark, he decided that they would allow double that to make sure they made it there in time. He wasn't sure what to bring as he had never had a rendezvous with kidnappers before. He decided a torch would probably be useful and having put the entire contents of the house back in its drawers, he was possibly the only person who knew exactly where to find one.

He made sure Dorene had visited the bathroom and asked her to put on one of Melanie's large fur coats, including a matching fur hat so that she wouldn't be cold. She looked like the wife of a Russian oligarch. There was no way he would risk leaving her on her own in the house and, in actual fact, he could do with some moral support in the task that awaited him.

They set off in the Nissan Micra, Dorene clutching the black handbag containing the money and Graham trying to interpret the satnav's directions. He eventually found the little track that led up the hill and drove up it in a gear that was embarrassingly low. He leaned forward as much as his physique would allow and squinted through the steamy windscreen trying to make sure he didn't hit a big pothole. They stopped at each turning, double checking that they were on the right route and to their relief the numerous road-closed signs seemed not to affect their journey. They continued up the hill for a couple of miles until finally the road was blocked and they had reached their destination. They were ten minutes early.

Graham turned the engine off and they were surrounded by darkness. They didn't notice the small dark figure that was hidden on the edge of the forestry plantation to the west of the road.

They hadn't waited long before they saw the headlights of a vehicle making its way up the hill. After about a minute a dark van pulled up about ten meters from Graham's Micra. There were muffled sounds coming from it and Graham wound the window down to try and hear better. It sounded like there was an argument going on. The van started maneuvering and was soon pointing the way it had come from. The doors opened and two figures, one tall, one short, came out wearing very bright head torches.

Graham opened the driver's door and got out and was quickly joined by Dorene. His own light was like a small candle in comparison and he struggled to see anything other than the two bright shiny spotlights in front of him. He heard one of the men address the other in Russian and leaned over towards Dorene and whispered "What did he say?"

"He said: 'OMG look at that fat fucker!'" Dorene replied without hesitation and Graham wished he hadn't asked. He felt totally disempowered when suddenly he heard Dorene shout something back at the men in Russian. The men's torches were suddenly facing each other and Graham could hear the short ugly one talk very quietly to the tall bearded man. He was just going to ask Dorene what she had said when the torches yet again were turned towards them and the bearded man shouted "Have you got the money?"

"Yes, we have," Graham shouted back and looked at Dorene who was still holding the black bag.

"Have you got Melanie with you?" he demanded.

"No. When we've counted the money we'll release her. Don't worry," the bearded man replied.

"How do we know you're telling the truth?" Graham asked, feeling a bit like a child questioning his parents whether stopping sucking his thumb will really make Santa give him big boys' presents.

"You'll have to take our word for it," the short man said and chuckled sarcastically.

Graham reached for the bag, but Dorene wouldn't hand it over to him. Instead, she strode confidently towards the bright lights of the two men and put the bag down at the feet of the taller one. He bent over to pick it up and Dorene placed a well-aimed kick into his face and spat in his direction before walking back to the Micra and getting into the passenger seat.

"You bitch!" the man shouted, still holding the bag

and covering his nose with his free hand.

"We'll release her soon. Expect a phone call," his companion added before both men got into the van and drove off.

Once the van had disappeared down the hill, Graham and Dorene were left in semi-darkness. Graham got back into the car and switched the engine on and nearly had a heart attack. In front of the car stood a boy that looked like he'd come straight from the Vietnam War. The boy walked up to the driver's side and Graham wound the window down in trepidation.

"Hi, I'm Josh. I've come in peace," the boy said and held his hand up showing his palm to emphasise what he had just said. "I've been told to tell ye to ignore the road closed signs. Just carry on straight and ye'll hit the main road and I'm coming with ye."

Graham was speechless but nodded to show he had understood. Josh retreated and moved the road closed sign to one side and then got into the back of the Micra.

"I suppose we'll drive home then," Graham said to Dorene, who nodded in agreement.

34

Tom and Josie waited in silence for Jack to come back. They had hidden Josie's bike in the ditch next to the road and were hunkered down out of sight, constantly slapping their necks and faces trying to kill the midges that were delighted at the new food source suddenly presented to them. Tom realised now why Jack had packed the mosquito head net.

Jack returned with the bikes, having skilfully ferried Josh's bike with his left hand down the hill. Jack put them in the ditch next to Josie's bike and waved for Tom to come over.

"Awricht, this is what ye gonnae do," Jack said like he was briefing an SAS team. "Josh's going to message me when the kidnappers are comin and tell us where the dosh is. Ye'll only have a few seconds to get it after they've stopped."

"How do you know they're going to stop?" Tom asked, starting to feel panicky.

"They gonnae stop awricht. Josie'll see to that." Even though it was very dark, Tom detected Jack's typical cheeky grin through the mosquito head net.

"And you?" Tom asked cautiously, not sure if he wanted to know.

"Ah'm gonnae make sure they won't be able to follow us!" came the reply which somewhat reassured

Tom even though he didn't know what this might involve.

They waited in the dark for what seemed like ages and Tom was getting seriously cold and irritated by the midges. No use complaining though. They eventually saw a pair of headlights further down the hill that slowly came nearer. Tom held his breath as the van drove past and continued up the hill. He glanced over to Josie and saw her starting to take her clothes off. He turned to Jack and made him look in Josie's direction.

"To make sure both of them get oot of the van. Ye got a betta idea?" Jack whispered in response.

Tom shook his head.

It didn't take long before Jack's phone vibrated.

"Awricht, the dosh's in a black handbag on the front passenger side. Got it?" Jack said to Tom, who nodded in response.

Josie put her clothes in a plastic shopping bag which she then stuffed in the kiddie trailer. She climbed out of the ditch with the moonlight illuminating her naked body as she gently tiptoed on the gravel-strewn surface to find a relatively clean-looking spot. Tom's trousers suddenly seemed tighter and he felt disturbed by the whole situation.

"How did you persuade Josie to do this?" Tom whispered to Jack.

"Ah didnae, she offered," Jack replied quietly.

Josie stretched out in the middle of the road and it didn't take long before they saw the headlights of a car coming down the hill. It looked like it was speeding up and Tom worried that they might not spot Josie. He was almost right. By the time they saw her, they had to slam the breaks on to stop in time. The van slid a good four meters on the loose gravel, before coming to a standstill a couple of meters from Josie's perfectly still and naked body.

It took a few seconds before either man moved, but as Jack predicted they both got out of the van with the engine left running to have a closer look.

As the two men walked up to Josie, Jack and Tom snuck up to the van. Thankfully the bearded man had left the passenger door open and it was an easy task to pull out the black handbag from the footwell. Tom felt his heart beat a million beats per minute as he retreated back into the dark ditch. From there he could see Jack crouching down for a few seconds by each wheel of the van. He soon joined Tom in the ditch and showed him three valves from the van's wheels.

"The caps will haud the air a wee bit, but after that, they're stuck urny gon anywhere. Make sure you're ready to scarper oan that bike," Jack whispered quietly before turning his attention to Josie. The two men had hunkered down next to her and looked unsure of what to do next. One of the men leant forward to check if she was breathing and this is when Josie opened her eyes and lifted her hand holding the small water pistol. She put a few well-aimed squirts in each man's eyes and quickly got up on her feet. The men were shouting and desperately trying to wipe the substance from under their eyelids, tears streaming down their faces. She quickly joined Tom and Jack and they got their bikes out of the ditch and set off down the hill. Josie, still naked, and Jack with the only torch lighting up the track just enough for them to find their way back towards the main road. Tom was too scared of crashing to take one of his hands off the handlebars to switch his own torch on.

Had they taken a moment to look back up the hill, they would have seen the van start to move and initially gain speed before starting to swerve erratically and then leave the road. Brief glimpses of the headlights would have indicated that it was tumbling down the heathery steep slope before coming to a standstill in the darkness. The headlights flickered for a few moments before going out altogether.

35

Josie put her clothes back on before they reached civilization and decided to head home to do some tidying before their parents arrived back from holiday. Tired and relieved, Tom and Jack pulled up outside Tom's house. Jack got the handbag out from the kiddie trailer and they walked through the front door in a triumphant fashion.

Tom looked around the living room to try and catch a glimpse of Melanie, but could only see Graham, Dorene and Josh. They were perched on the sofa in a way that indicated something wasn't right.

"Is Melanie not here?" Tom asked.

"No, they didn't bring her," Graham replied. "They promised they'd release her as soon as they've counted the money."

Jack stared angrily at Josh, who shrugged his shoulders as if to say "your fault for not asking". He then looked at Graham and slowly revealed the bag he had been holding behind his back and said "Sorry, we didn't know."

Graham's face turned white and he asked where they got the bag from. Tom and Jack told Graham and Dorene most of what had happened that evening, leaving out the bit about Josie being naked.

"Ah'm very sorry. We just wanted tae help," Jack

apologised and first looked at Graham, who didn't say anything and then at Dorene.

"Yes, dear. We know. They'll be in touch soon. I'm sure they don't want to keep Melanie for much longer. She can be quite hard work you know," Dorene said in a comforting voice.

Graham got up from the sofa and took the bag off Jack. He glanced inside it to make sure the money was still there.

"Shall we phone them up and explain?" Dorene asked Graham.

"No," Graham answered, "that would make us look like we were involved in stealing the money off them. Best to lie low and wait for them to contact us."

Jack made his excuses and left with Josh. Tom joined Dorene to watch a film about artificial insemination of racing camels in Saudi Arabia but wasn't really paying much attention. Graham found himself pacing nervously for the first time in his life and didn't enjoy it much. The phone didn't ring.

They eventually went to bed.

At daybreak the doorbell chimed repeatedly, accompanied by loud knocks on the front door. Graham was in the en-suite bathroom and wished Tom would go and answer the door, but judging by the repeated knocking, that wasn't happening. Graham went downstairs and opened the door fraction of a second before realising that it could have been the Russians coming to take revenge. Thankfully on the other side was the Asian officer Graham recognized from the golf club earlier in the week.

"PC Akram. Can I come in please?" the officer asked.

Graham brought him through to the dining area and as usual no coffee or tea was required.

"Before I tell you why I'm here, I'd just like to check if you have had any news from Melanie since yesterday?" PC Akram asked and looked intensely at Graham.

Graham was happy to be able to answer truthfully that, no, he hadn't heard from Melanie and that he was getting increasingly concerned. He then noticed that the black handbag was on the dining table, within easy reach of the officer and he tried his best not to look at it.

"Last night we picked up a signal from her phone again. This time we tracked it down to an area north of here. Quite a remote place actually. Being Saturday night we didn't have a patrol car to send immediately, and the location of the signal wasn't moving, so it wasn't until a few hours later we managed to send some officers over to check it out." PC Akram stopped as he had noticed that Graham kept glancing at the bag next to him. "Is this Melanie's bag?" he asked.

Graham reached across the officer, grabbed the bag, and said "No, it is my mother's, and she is looking for it upstairs. I'll just pop up with it for her. She's got dementia and can get quite agitated." The young officer nodded sympathetically.

Graham took the bag upstairs and hid it under his bed. He quickly glanced into Dorene's bedroom to make sure she was still asleep, which she thankfully was, and returned to officer Akram downstairs.

"Sorry about that," Graham apologized, feeling quite pleased with his quick thinking.

"So, I've only come on shift just now but I was told in our morning briefing that they found a van that had come off the road. It matched the description of the vehicle seen by your neighbour and had two recently deceased males inside it. We believe they died from the injuries sustained in the crash, but only the post mortem will tell us for sure. We found Melanie's phone in one of the men's coat pockets but no sign of Melanie unfortunately. The vehicle is undergoing a forensic examination to see what might have happened. I can't go into details but there were signs of tampering with the vehicle that may well have resulted in the accident." PC Akram paused, then stood up.

"Do you have any idea where she might be?" Graham asked as he followed the officer out into the hallway.

"Not yet. But now we know who might have been involved in her disappearance. That should at least give us some more ideas of where to search," the officer replied and promised to keep Graham updated with any developments before leaving.

Graham returned to the kitchen and put the coffee machine on. He hadn't even had breakfast and things were going from bad to worse. If the kidnappers were dead, who knew where Melanie was being held? And had his nephew and his friend committed a double murder?

Tom walked into the kitchen and opened the fridge. "Any news?" he asked Graham.

Graham put the packet of coffee beans down and after a slight pause said "We might have a problem."

* * *

Tom brought a bowl of cereal up to his bedroom. He got back in bed and shovelled spoonfuls of cornflakes into his mouth, trying to make sense of what Graham had just told him. He began thinking about what might happen to Melanie but was soon worrying about his own future. He wasn't the one who had removed the tyre valves, but even so, he had been part of the plan that had killed two people. Not nice ones, but the police weren't going to ignore a double murder just because the men were criminals. At least he hadn't left any fingerprints and was pretty sure there hadn't been any witnesses. He phoned Jack after checking a couple of websites for news about the accident.

"Awricht ye bampot!" Jack answered. "Any news about Melanie?"

Tom told Jack what he had just found out from Graham while trying to conceal how worried he was.

"This isnae real," Jack replied. "Ah'd better get rid of the valves then. They're still in me pocket! And Josie said she must've dropped the water pistol, ye know, the one with the vinegar in it, when she got her bike oot of the ditch. Did the polis say anything aboot that?" For once Jack sounded quite concerned.

"Don't know," Tom replied, now feeling even worse than before.

"Ye still got the dosh, right?" Jack asked.

"I think so," Tom answered.

"Git ower 'ere and bring the bag with ye. Ah'll look up flights to South America," Jack announced, to which Tom exclaimed

"What!"

"Just joshing! But seriously, ye should make sure the polis don't find the dosh. I'd be happy to look after it for ye," Jack told Tom, who had thought the same thing, but felt that Jack would probably be the last person he'd trust with fifty grand.

"No, I'm going to go to my mom's, I've got college tomorrow," Tom replied before hanging up.

Exactly a week ago his mum had told him that his dad had died. He'd hardly seen her since but he realised now that all he wanted to do was sit on the sofa at home and watch Midsomer Murders on the TV with her and for everything to be back to normal. He hadn't even had time to tell her that Melanie had been kidnapped.

36

Melanie's wrists were swollen and the zip ties had started to cut into her skin. The two men had visited twice. The first time they had given her another banana and the second time some water and a sausage roll, which she had eaten with some reservations. She had also been allowed to use a bucket. That was a long time ago now. Melanie had been asleep and was sure it must be the next morning and still nobody had come back. Knowing that the bucket was there, made her feel reluctant to wet her trousers again so she continued holding it in.

The feeling that something must have gone wrong kept growing. Did anyone know where she was or was she going to be left there to die? In the past, she had frequently fantasised about her own death. She had been torn between dying young and attractive or old and wizened but, as it was a fantasy after all, decided it would be old and attractive. More than likely her gorgeous lover would be holding her hand, begging her to cling on as he wouldn't be able to carrry on living without her. She'd be lying in an antique French bed, with pristine white bed linen, in a large airy room with tall Georgian windows. The sunlight would suddenly stream in, hitting her face just as she drew her last breath.

She now feared dying alone, lying in her own piss and shit in the dark. And she had to admit, kidnapping aside, that this was more likely than any other scenario.

She suddenly went into survival-mode and managed to get to her feet. Standing up while being hungry and dehydrated after so many hours of lying down had made her feel very dizzy. She had to bend over for a good thirty seconds to let the blood reach her brain. Once she felt stable on her feet, she gently shuffled sideways in the darkness until she felt the cold wall with her shoulder. She started working her way along the wall using her body to detect anything that could help her either remove the zip tie from her wrists or get the hood off her head. After a minute she bumped into something that felt like a hook. It was at shoulder height so she managed to position the hood on the edge of the hook and pull her head out, thankful that the Russians had become sloppier each time they had put it back on her head and not closed the drawstring very tight around her neck. It was a relief to be able to draw a breath of relatively fresh air, albeit only through her nose.

She looked around and she could see daylight in the gaps around the garage door. She was right, it was the next day. She saw the bucket, still with the previous day's content sitting in a corner. She tried her best to pull her trousers down with her hands tied behind her back but soon had to give up. Having no other choice she crouched down over the bucket regardless, even though her trousers seem to absorb most of it.

She was now able to think more clearly and looked around the garage. She knew already that it was pretty empty. Apart from the bucket and the hook on the wall, there was a single light bulb hanging in the ceiling, but no windows. She decided to make use of the hook to try and snap the zip tie but her hands weren't able to reach the hook despite her standing on her toes. She wished she had persevered with her yoga classes. The only thing she could stand on was the bucket and she moved it using her feet to the round drain located in the middle of the floor and knocked it over with her foot, letting the content find its way through the grate covering the circular hole. She flicked the bucket upside down and positioned it below the hook. When standing on it she was just able to put the hook between her hands. She made sure the zip tie was caught by the hook as she lowered her body down. Nothing happened apart from that she now was hanging painfully off the hook. She put her feet back on the bucket while leaving her hands still in contact with the hook and then in a suicidal fashion kicked the bucket to one side. The hook suddenly took all the weight, the tie snapped and she landed face-first on the concrete floor. Her nose was bleeding and her front teeth were hurting but that was nothing compared to the relief at finally having full use of her arms. She gently pulled the tape off her mouth.

She walked up to the aluminium roller door and was tempted to start banging on it, but she had seen too many films where the kidnappers had returned just as everyone thought the heroine was about to succeed in her escape. Instead, she grabbed the door by the bottom edge but only managed to lift it an inch off the ground. Peering out she could see a small padlock securing the door to a bracket on the ground. She let go and the door closed again, having let in just enough light to make her unable to see much in the dark. She thought for a moment and then lifted the round cast iron metal grate from the drain in the floor. It was about eight inches across and reassuringly heavy. She propped the door up on the edge of her foot and repeatedly hit the padlock with the heavy grate. The rusty bracket gave way and she was able to roll the door up and exit the garage. She closed it again behind her and ran off and hid amongst some shrubs twenty meters away. She waited there for a few minutes to gather her thoughts.

She had no idea where she was. It looked like a housing estate with a mix of flats and semi-detected little houses. They looked reasonably newly built but were rather cheap and uninspiring. She was pretty sure she had never been here before. If she had her phone, she could called an Uber to take her home to clean herself up, before calling the police. She really looked dreadful. Her hair was matted and greasy. Her light blue jumper had stains of blood and dirt on it. She had a big rip in her jeans where it wasn't trendy to have a cut and she reeked of stale urine. She couldn't tell what her face looked like but suspected there was blood all over it because she could taste it when running her tongue over her lips. She looked like a homeless druggie.

She saw a woman pushing a pram and ran out from the bush waving her hands to get the woman's attention.

"Can I use your phone please?" Melanie called out.

The woman started walking faster, ignoring Melanie's plea for help.

Melanie was shocked by the woman's reaction and started walking the opposite way towards a row of shops she could see in the distance. A young man wearing a grey tracksuit was walking towards her but crossed the road as soon he spotted her. Melanie shouted angrily at him, but he kept on walking, not even looking Melanie's way.

She noticed a rough-looking gentleman smoking outside the bookies, the type of guy she normally would have given a wide berth. She was about to ask him for help when he said "Sorry love, haven't got any change," and put his cigarette out and went back inside the betting shop.

This is ridiculous Melanie thought. Nobody will even tell me where I am. Even as she stood in front of the shops, people were walking past her like she was invisible and she felt like crying.

"Can someone phone the police!" she shouted and looked around. Two teenage girls were staring at her with pity in their eyes, whispering to each other. An old lady pushing a three-wheeled rollator came up from behind and said "Would you mind stepping aside my love? You are blocking the pavement."

Melanie went into the nearest shop which happened to be a newsagent. She approached the lady behind the counter at the back and told her to watch as she went up to the magazine racks.

"Look!" Melanie shouted. "Look at me! I'm taking these magazines. And I'm not gonna pay for them." Melanie tried to keep eye contact while she picked up a random bundle of men's motor magazines that happened to be closest. "Call the police!" she added to get her point across. The woman behind the counter, who must have been around her own age, looked at her with tired eyes but made no effort to call anyone. At this point, Melanie lost it and started grabbing magazines by the handful and throwing them on the floor. She swept whole boxes of sweets off the shelves while screaming at the top of her voice.

The lady eventually got her mobile out and dialled a number.

Melanie stopped and looked at the woman intensely. "I hope for your sake that's the police you're calling." The woman, who now looked slightly scared, nodded, and then said "Police please."

37

Graham sat at the breakfast bar in the kitchen with his second cup of coffee that had now gone cold. He couldn't remember ever feeling this stressed and that was despite years of bullying at school. It was gone eleven and another wave of anxiety grew from his stomach and sent waves of tingling through the rest of his body when he realized that Dorene hadn't yet resurfaced. He walked up the stairs, each step with increasing anxiety, and peeked into her bedroom for the second time that morning. She wasn't in her bed and Graham was both relieved and unsettled by this.

"I'm in here!" he heard from another room that turned out to be Stuart's office when Graham gently pushed the door fully open. He saw his mother sitting at Stuart's desk, still wearing her nightgown, writing on a piece of paper. "I'll be down shortly, just need to finish this while I remember what I wanted to write," she said and looked up and smiled.

Graham had returned downstairs and put the kettle on again when Tom came down with the empty cereal bowl, which he placed on the kitchen worktop.

"I'm going to my mum's, is that ok?" he asked Graham.

"Yes, of course," Graham replied. "I wish I could take you, but I can't risk leaving Grandma on her own."

"I'll be fine. I'll take the bus," Tom replied and Graham could see how worried he looked. Gone was the usual jokey banter and he wouldn't even look Graham in the eyes. Graham realized that he wasn't the only one feeling extremely anxious.

He walked up to Tom and put his arms around him. Tom wasn't exactly hugging him back but he didn't withdraw from the embrace either. They stood like that in silence for a minute until Graham took a step back and got Tom to look at him.

"Listen, we'll sort this. Don't worry. Forget about what has just happened. The police know who these guys are, they'll be able to find Melanie now. I won't say anything to the police about what you did last night. I've not told them about me and Dorene being there either or that they had demanded a ransom of us. As far as they know, we were never there. We weren't in any way involved in this whole thing," Graham explained trying to reassure Tom.

Tom looked at Graham and then burst into tears.

"It's not just that. I think I might also have killed my dad," Tom replied as large tears rolled down his face. Between sobs, he told Graham about the small bag of ketamine he'd given his dad last time he'd seen him. Graham's face contorted in pain and he could see Tom looking confused. He wanted to tell him not to worry, but he felt like he couldn't breathe. It felt like an elephant had suddenly sat on his ribcage preventing him from getting any air. Pain was building in his chest and he started to feel dizzy. His skin felt damp with moisture oozing out from his pores like someone squeezing a cold and wet kitchen sponge and he sat down on a chair to take the weight off his trembling legs.

"Call an ambulance. I think I'm having a heart attack," he managed to whisper to Tom.

38

The police seemed to take ages to arrive, which meant that Melanie stood awkwardly for a long time in the mess she had created in the newsagent. She had calmed down after someone had finally listened to her plea for help. She started to put the magazines back on the racks and pick up some of the sweet packets off the floor while trying to explain to the lady behind the counter that she had been the victim of a kidnapping. The woman's face gave no clues as to whether she believed her or not.

Two uniformed police officers eventually arrived and immediately walked up and addressed Melanie in a way that made her realize how scary it felt to be subjected to institutional prejudice. She replied politely to their questions and they quickly softened their stance and listened carefully to what she had to say. She was in no doubt helped by her relatively sophisticated accent. They consulted someone on the radio to verify her information and started treating her like a victim, rather than a criminal. Even the woman behind the counter started showing some sympathy and declined to take the matter of vandalism any further.

She had preferred to go home to clean herself up, but the police officers insisted that she'd go with them to the station, where they would take her statement and collect any forensic evidence. But first, they asked her to point out where she had been kept hostage, which involved a slight detour via the row of garages.

At the police station, she declined to see a doctor and instead asked for some food and water. She was given a plastic triangular packet containing a cheese sandwich that must have come out of a vending machine and a bag of prawn cocktail crisps. Even though she was starving she didn't enjoy eating either item. She was then asked to wait in a bland room with utilitarian furniture. She became acutely aware of her own smell and tried to sit as still as possible to not waft it around too much. First came the photographer, who took pictures of her face and she felt compelled to clarify that the injuries to her lip and nose were caused by her escaping rather than by the kidnappers. Apart from the marks left by the zip ties on her wrists, she had no other visible injuries and the photographer soon left. She was then asked if she wished to see a councillor to help her psychologically, but she said that she would prefer to go home as soon as possible. She was assured that an officer would come and take her statement soon and she would then be taken home.

When she was finally interviewed, she described in brief sentences what had happened. There wasn't much to say really, as she had spent the last forty-eight hours mostly in darkness with a hood over her head, but she gave as thorough description of the kidnappers as she could. The policewoman then showed her the note with threats that they had found which Melanie realized she had almost forgotten about. She was surprised when the female officer started asking her questions about her personal life, more specifically if she was having an affair. Melanie said no, but the officer wouldn't move on and asked more explicitly if she had been seeing Mike next door. Melanie looked in some disbelief at the officer, who added that allegedly Mike had smelt of her perfume on more than one occasion. Melanie got irritated and started wondering if she was on the Jeremy Kyle show. This was getting ridiculous.

"I hug people, especially if I'm being comforted by them because my husband has died or my mother-in-law is connected to a heart and lung machine," Melanie said. "That is probably why Mike smelt of my perfume and no other reason."

"OK, fair enough," the policewoman said. "We know who sent you the note. This person has been in our custody and is now released on bail. We suspected she might have something to do with your abduction and the damage caused to your property."

The penny dropped and Melanie realized that they were referring to Helen and it all made sense now. That sad and bitter woman. Melanie almost felt she shouldn't exonerate Helen, but it sounded like she had suffered enough. Melanie explained that her husband had borrowed money from some dubious characters to get out of a bad property deal and that she was pretty sure that these people were the ones who had abducted her.

"Well it looks like you have no need to worry about them anymore," the police officer said almost cheerfully. "They have both died in a car accident so shouldn't trouble you anymore."

At least that explained why they never returned, Melanie thought.

"How do you know they were the people that kidnapped me?" Melanie then asked the officer.

"Ah, yes," the officer replied, "we found them because we picked up the signal from your mobile phone. And as your description matches very well with their appearance, we are now pretty sure they are the people that abducted you."

"Can I have my phone back?" Melanie asked. "I've got a lot of things I need to sort out, such as my husband's funeral."

"Unfortunately, your phone is now evidence and we can't give it back to you yet. You'd better off getting a new one for the time being. Sorry." The female officer seemed pretty callous about it and announced it in a way that indicated that it wasn't up for negotiation. She turned a piece of paper over and resumed the interview.

"Do you know what these men were doing on the moor yesterday evening?" she asked.

"No idea," Melanie said after a moment's hesitation. She didn't want to drag Graham into this if she didn't have to.

"We have evidence that their accident was caused by someone tampering with their vehicle," the officer asked and looked at Melanie with a mix of suspicion and hope.

"Well, it wasn't me. I'm sure they had plenty of enemies," Melanie answered while trying to keep calm. "Can I go home now?"

She was escorted to a police car and a junior officer was asked to take her home. She sat in the backseat and wondered what had happened the previous night. Graham didn't seem like the kind of guy who would mess with someone's vehicle. She didn't want to be judgmental but she also thought it was unlikely Graham had fifty grand to pay the ransom with. Maybe there was more to Graham than she had first thought?

Just as the police car was about to turn into Kilmardinny Gardens an ambulance pulled out and Melanie could hear the sirens as it rapidly disappeared out of view. She was dropped off outside her house and walked onto the drive in time to see Dorene get into Graham's car with Tom standing in the doorway.

"Melanie!" Tom exclaimed. Melanie had never seen Tom so happy to see her and it warmed her heart. She was also quite happy to see him, she had to admit. Thankfully he didn't seem keen to hug her and instead started to talk at a hundred miles an hour.

"Graham's ill, he's having a heart attack, the ambulance came, and now Grandma wants to drive to the hospital..." Tom held up the car keys showing that at least one danger had been averted. Dorene had at this point spotted Melanie and got out of the car.

"Melanie, what's happened to you, dear?" Dorene looked at Melanie's dishevelled state, her own appearance, in a beige pleated skirt and light mauve cardigan, being that of a neat school teacher. Melanie didn't know which level to start at and decided to ignore Dorene and walk past Tom into the house. "Look after your grandma, I need a shower."

Melanie wished she could have soaked in the bath to recover from the last two days but had to make do with a very quick hose down instead. She quickly towelled her hair and used a hair bobble to scrunch it all up into a messy ball on top of her head. She quickly put on some clean clothes and went downstairs without any makeup. She couldn't remember the last time she had left the house without wearing makeup. How things had changed in just a week.

Tom and Dorene were standing at the bottom of the stairs like attentive dogs worried someone might go for a walk without them. She grabbed a coat and her handbag and said "Ok let's all go," finishing the statement with a slight sigh. Now was not a time to be precious about her car, she tried to tell herself.

39

The aggressively healthy-looking paramedic attached sticky patches on Graham's chest as the ambulance left Kilmardinny Gardens. Graham looked grey and sweat was dripping off his chin and he felt like illness personified next to the young fit man, busy with trying to collect electrical currents off his large chest. The unit seemed to malfunction a couple of times and beeped with a frequency that was impossible to ignore. The paramedic, wearing a badge saying Jonathan, adjusted a couple of the sticky patches and pressed a few buttons on the ECG machine which made it sound happier. It wasn't long before they arrived at the Queen Elizabeth, a place Graham started to become very familiar with. As the ambulance pulled up to the A&E entrance, Graham started to feel a bit better. His heart was no longer racing uncontrollably and he felt able to breathe more easily. He offered to walk himself in, rather than be confined to the trolley, hoping to ease the workload of the ambulance crew.

"No chance," Jonathan replied, "last time someone did that we had to get the fire brigade to help us get them off the floor. You'd better stick to the trolley, sorry mate."

Graham wasn't sure how offended he should be, but didn't feel he was in a position to argue about it. Maybe

Jonathan had a point after all.

He was rolled into the A&E department and passed some of the stragglers sleeping off the previous night's drinking and fighting sessions. He could even smell the stale booze in the air. Thankfully he was quickly transferred to a bed, which meant shuffling across from one trolley on wheels to another, while the ambulance crew was waiting to get the equipment back. The curtains were drawn and he found himself alone with a very large and smiley nurse. He was quite surprised that nurses' uniforms were available in such large sizes. She had big frizzy red hair and a mouth wide enough to take a Mars bar sideways. If her head had been that of a slim person her mouth wouldn't have fitted on her face. Her name badge had stickers of little flowers on it and you could just make out that it said Veronica. She put some sticky electrodes on his chest and, due to being quite short, had to stretch awkwardly across him to get them in the correct position. He could feel the warmth of her body and the smell of her hair. Graham surprised himself by experiencing a wave of desire, which he was pretty certain wasn't a symptom of a heart attack. Actually, he was starting to feel a whole lot better and said as much to the nurse.

"Ah'm sooo happy to hear that," she replied in a truly delightful way, free from any sarcasm. "Ah'm just gonnae take a wee bit of blood just in case," she continued and reached for a kidney-shaped paper dish containing a needle and test tubes. Graham caught sight of the needle and promptly fainted.

She felt the nurse tapping his hand gently saying "Mr

Firth, are ye awricht? Donnae like the needle?"

"No, I don't do needles," Graham confessed after the blood had returned to his brain.

"Nuthin to be scared off. Who's gonnae be a big boy now?" Veronica said as she gently rubbed the crease of Graham's elbow with an antiseptic wipe. He looked away as she skillfully filled three test tubes and finished the procedure by putting a little plaster on Graham's skin.

"The doctor will see ye soon. Just give us a wee shout if ye need anything," Veronica said before disappearing behind the curtain.

Graham didn't exactly feel well, but certainly didn't feel at death's door anymore. The last time he'd had his blood taken was when he was twelve and Dorene had taken him and his brother to the doctor's. He had fainted then as well and done his best to avoid seeing a doctor ever since. He expected he'd be told off once the tests came back. At least the machine next to him was obediently bleeping away, plotting nice and even traces on the monitor. Not being able to see anything apart from the curtains around his bed made him listen harder to what was going on around him.

Something must have happened as suddenly there was cooing and cheering from all the nurses. Their joy was polarizing and Graham immediately felt left out, not knowing what the occasion was. He could do with a bit of good news for a change.

After a minute the joyful laughter subsided and Veronica returned and opened the curtain revealing Tom, Dorene, and not at least Melanie.

"Looks like ye got some visitors?" Veronica announced. "Dinnae know Dorene's yer maw! She's our hero. A true champion!" and with that Veronica left the cubicle leaving ample space for the others to get close to Graham's bed.

"Melanie! You are free!" Graham exclaimed. "What happened?" he said and looked closely at the bruising on Melanie's face.

Melanie self-consciously put her hand up to hide her nose and upper lip.

"I'll tell you later. More importantly, how are you?" she asked with genuine concern.

"I thought I was having a heart attack, but I'm not so sure now. I feel a lot better," Graham replied and smiled, looking almost embarrassed.

A head appeared in the gap of the curtain belonging to Dr McTavish, the young heavily tattooed doctor who had looked after Dorene.

"Oh, hello Dorene, didn't expect to see you here! How are you doing?" Dr McTavish addressed Dorene, who blushed like a young girl.

"Oh, I'm fine now. It is my son who is poorly. Do you know what is wrong with him?" Dorene asked the doctor and Graham felt like he was about five years old again. It was strangely comforting to let his mum do the talking.

"Nothing wrong with him at all!" Dr MacTavish replied and turned to Graham. "We've done the blood tests and a cardiologist had a look at the ECG. There're no signs of a myocardial infarction at all. Basically, you've not had a heart attack. Actually, both your blood pressure and cholesterol are lower than average for your age. I'm thinking it's mostly likely you had a panic attack. Is this the first time this has happened?"

Graham nodded his head in response.

"Have you been under pressure recently?" the doctor asked, to which Dorene exclaimed "Pressure! I'll tell you about pressure. We had the worst week you can ever imagine, I think I wouldn't even notice having a panic attack, had one smacked me in the face. To be honest I can't wait to get back to the old wrinkly home to get some rest and I'm sure Graham feels exactly the same!" In the wake of her energetic outburst, they all could hear a trickle as a puddle was forming on the floor between Dorene's legs.

Graham nodded in agreement with an apologetic smile.

"Yes, it has been a rather stressful week," he told the doctor.

"Here's a leaflet about panic attacks to help you, should it happen again," Dr MacTavish said and handed Graham a piece of paper. "One of the nurses will come and clean up and get you unhooked from the monitors so you can go home. Nice to meet you all again." And with that, the young doctor left the cubicle.

Within half an hour they were all in Melanie's car on their way home.

40

Back at Eagle's Nest Manor the mood was celebratory. Tom and Melanie were preparing a roast chicken dinner in the kitchen and Graham could hear them laughing as they were teasing each other about the things they liked and didn't like to eat.

Graham was told to rest on the sofa and Tom made sure there were cold beer and snacks at hand. Graham had answered "You know me, Tom. If I can reach it, I'll eat it", to Tom's offer of refreshments and Tom had interpreted it as to keep the snacks coming for his uncle.

Dorene came down and looked at Graham with a serious face, which at once made Graham feel uneasy.

"I just want to give you this," she said and handed him a pale envelope with A. Zoransky written on it in old-fashioned handwriting. "If you decide to find him, please give him this letter. It will make him understand."

Graham looked at the letter and eventually said "Thank you." He hadn't had time to fully ponder whether to do anything with the newly gained knowledge about his heritage, but knowing he had his mother's blessing would at least take one stressful aspect out of the equation.

"Dinner's ready," Tom called from the dining area and Graham and Dorene joined the others, feeling that this particular discussion should remain a secret between the two of them until Graham decided otherwise.

* * *

After the very late Sunday lunch, Dorene and Graham cleared the table while Melanie, not having her phone to hand, sat and looked out through the patio doors. At the bottom of the garden, the ash tree was displaying plenty of yellow leaves and she noticed the barbeque was still out. She ought to put that away for the winter.

They all jumped when the doorbell rang.

"I'll get it," they heard Tom shout from the living room.

Moments later, a stocky middle-aged police officer with fashionable stubble walked into the dining area.

"Sorry to disturb you this late Sunday afternoon. I just wanted to give Melanie her phone back as I know she sadly has many things to arrange and we have got what we needed from it," he said and handed the phone over to Melanie, who looked very appreciative.

"Would you like a coffee?" Graham asked out of habit and was surprised to hear the officer accept the offer.

"Milk, two sugars, please," he added.

Graham put the coffee machine on, after making sure the officer didn't mind waiting for it to warm up. Proper coffee after all was worth waiting for.

"You'll be pleased to know that the case of the Russians has been more or less solved," the officer told them as Tom joined the group and sat down next to his grandma.

"Ooo, so what happened?" Dorene asked with a twinkle in her eye. Graham felt nervous and hoped she wouldn't say anything that would seem suspicious.

"I'm not sure I should tell you the details really, as we're still investigating, but we received an anonymous tipoff late this morning about some Albanians over in Springburn. We actually found the tyre valves from the van when we raided their car wash. Amazing. You'd think they would have had the sense to throw them away, wouldn't you?! Anyway, it all fits as these guys have been our main suspects in a sex trafficking ring for a while. You had a lucky escape!" the policeman said and looked at Melanie.

Tom sniggered and Melanie turned towards him looking offended.

"What, you think I'm not attractive enough to be sex trafficked? Is that what's so funny?" she asked and Tom just smiled back, trying not to laugh.

"Where has the sugar gone?" Graham asked Melanie, partly as a way of changing the subject.

"In the blue jar," she replied and pointed to a shelf.

Graham lifted the lid and saw it was empty.

"Anymore anywhere?" he asked Melanie.

She joined Graham in the kitchen and started looking in the cupboards.

"It's not important. I can manage without," the officer said.

"I've found some sugar upstairs. I'll go and get it." Dorene said quietly to Tom and disappeared up the stairs.

Less than a minute later Tom caught sight of Dorene, just before she entered the kitchen. She was holding a small clear bag with a white powder and, like a ninja, he blocked the doorway to prevent her from entering. He grabbed the bag from her hand and put his finger up to his mouth to indicate to Dorene to be quiet. Thankfully the policeman was admiring the coffee machine while Graham was noisily grinding some beans so nobody had noticed Tom's panicked actions. He immediately went to the downstairs loo and flushed the contents of the plastic bag down the toilet. He rinsed the bag thoroughly before putting it into the small metal bin under the washbasin. He felt relief and fear in equal measures and returned to the kitchen in time to watch the police officer pour beautiful foamed milk hearts into a couple of cups of double espressos.

"I wasn't always a policeman," the officer said jokingly. After finishing his coffee, he bid the family farewell and said that he hoped they'd never meet again. A joke, they could tell, he had told a thousand times before.

41

They all flopped on the sofas in front of the TV watching Blue Planet. Nobody had the energy to talk. Dorene had fallen asleep and was quietly snoring away, Graham wasn't far from drifting off himself when he felt Tom tug at his arm. Tom leant forward and whispered into Graham's ear "What are we going to do about the money?"

Graham became wide awake again. The money! He'd totally forgotten about the money. He told Tom to wait and went upstairs. He returned with the black handbag and handed it to Melanie, who looked confused. She opened the bag and pulled out a bundle of cash.

"What is this?" she asked and looked first at Graham and then at Tom.

"Isn't it yours?" Graham answered.

"I don't think so. I mean, where did you find it? In this bag?" she asked.

"No, it was inside the piano. We were going to use it to pay the ransom. There's fifty grand in there," Graham explained.

"I see, but the kidnappers never made it," Melanie said.

Graham was tempted to leave it at that, as there was no need for Melanie to know what had actually happened.

"Oh no, we gave it to the kidnappers," Dorene said, having just woken up in time to see Melanie pull the money out of the bag.

Melanie looked confused. Graham sighed.

"My friends and I got the money back," Tom filled in. "But we didn't mean to kill them. That wasn't really part of the plan and not really our fault."

"I thought the Albanians had done that!? I don't want to hear anymore," Melanie said and shook her head. She now looked distinctly worried. After a brief pause, she continued "The money must be what Stuart owed the Russians. But it was inside the piano so he must have meant for you to have it, Graham." She put the bundle of twenties back inside and put the bag on the floor in front of Graham.

Graham stood in silence for a minute, while everyone waited for his response.

"You know what. I think it's best that we split the money between us. We've all played a part in this and I think that it's probably what Stuart would have wanted," Graham said and looked at the others. They all nodded in agreement. It did indeed sound like the best option.

"Count me out of it," Dorene said. "I'd probably just have to use it for care home fees anyway. To be honest, what I'd really like is for the piano to come back with me to Silver Angels. Just for a little while."

"Mum, it would be a pleasure to arrange. I'm sick of tuning their old one anyway. You can keep the piano for as long as you like, it's yours despite what the will said," Graham replied before asking rhetorically "Ok, what's fifty divided by three."

"Can we give something to Jack?" Tom interrupted cautiously. "I mean, he's the one who got the money back for us. I would never have thought of doing that."

Graham had to agree, not to give Jack something would be unfair considering that he also seemed to have cleaned up the mess he'd caused. Let's hope the Albanians actually were bad guys and never found out who'd stitched them up.

"Ok then. How about fifteen for each one of us and that leaves five for Jack. Sounds ok?" Graham said and looked first at Melanie and then at Tom. Both nodded approvingly in response. "Well, that's that settled then."

Tom took the bag and started to divide up the cash. He wasn't going to risk anyone changing their minds. He took one of the three big bundles and held up a smaller amount in his other hand. "I'll give this to Jack after college tomorrow," Tom said and left the living room.

In the hall, he stopped and shouted "Melanie, I forgot to say there's a letter for you here."

"It's ok, I'll come and get it." Melanie got up and it took a long time before she came back to the living room. When she did, she had tears streaming down her face but seemed calm and even managed a gentle smile.

"It's from the coroner," she announced to Graham and Dorene, who both looked very concerned. "It's about Stuart. They finally got the autopsy through," Melanie said and wiped her tears with the back of her hand. She sat down next to Graham and showed him the letter.

Graham read parts of it aloud for Dorene's benefit. "Cause of death... massive myocardial infarction due to familial hypercholesterolemia... No action required... can be released for burial..."

"So it was a heart attack after all," Graham said and turned to face Melanie.

She nodded. She was still rubbing the skin below her eyes as if to wipe off any smudges from the mascara she wasn't actually wearing.

"Well, we all knew that," Dorene exclaimed with the emphasis on that. Both Graham and Melanie looked at her. "What do you mean?" Graham asked his mother.

"I'm amazed he made it into his fifties, to be honest. I'm glad he did of course. Your dad sadly died in his early forties as you know. Which is why we found out that Stuart also had it. He worked so hard looking after himself and was so strict with what he ate. I got that drummed into him when he was little. That and the benefits of modern drugs of course," Dorene said as if she was speaking to herself.

"I still don't know what you're on about mum," Graham said. "You mean you knew he'd have a heart attack?"

"He had very high cholesterol. Genetic. Didn't he tell you?" Dorene looked at Graham and then Melanie and by the looks on their faces she gathered that he hadn't told them.

"He probably wouldn't have wanted you to worry about him," Dorene said and sighed.

She looked up and said "But at least you didn't get it, Graham. So dad not being your actual dad was a good thing! Wasn't it?"

This time it was Melanie who said "What do you mean?" as she looked in astonishment at Dorene.

Graham looked at his mum and shrugged his shoulders to say that it no longer mattered who knew. They told Melanie about Dorene's past.

42

It had rained most of the morning like it always seemed to do in late October. But just as the small group arrived at the golf club car park, streaks of pale sunshine managed to break through the dark and heavy clouds. Tom was wearing his new black shoes and the black shirt, the same clothes as he had worn for the service at the crematorium the week before. Melanie looked like she was on a photoshoot for the Dolce & Gabbana widow collection and had taken precautions by using waterproof mascara. Graham and Dorene were underdressed style-wise but at least felt warm and comfortable. Melanie was carrying Stuart's ashes in a modern and plain-looking urn inside the now-famous black handbag.

"Are you sure she knows we're coming?" Melanie asked Tom.

"'Course she does. I spoke to her an hour ago. She's meeting us here," Tom answered and scanned the car park.

"Do we know which hole we need to go to? I just hope it isn't too far away. These are suede stiletto-heeled boots. I don't want to be trekking across mud just because Stuart got a hole in one once!" Melanie said and sounded irritable. "And in any case, has Josie got permission from the golf club for this? I mean, it might have consequences for the other players, affect the putting or something. I don't know."

Josie, Jack, and Josh appeared, looking as smart as Tom had ever seen them. He felt touched that they had made the effort.

"Awricht, ye numpty!" Jack greeted Tom and they all gathered together.

"Josie, I believe Tom told you what Stuart's will said. I hope his request hasn't caused too much inconvenience for you," Graham said slightly nervously.

"No, it's fine. Ah have to admit it took me a wee while to remember," Josie replied and everyone could see the worry that suddenly came over Melanie's face. "Ah didnae know much aboot his golfing as ah only saw him in the bar," Josie continued.

"Is that the famous watering hole that he might have referred to?" Dorene asked, sounding hopeful that she had figured it out. "Does he want to sit inside that urn at the bar for all eternity?"

"No, his favourite hole is that one," Josie said and pointed to the VIP car park entrance where there was a deep pothole that was almost full of water from the rain that morning.

Melanie looked at the hole and then back at Josie. "Surely you're joking? Why would that be his favourite hole?"

They all looked at the pothole trying to make sense of it when an Audi A4 hit the hole splashing a golfer wearing perfectly ironed beige golfing trousers as he left the car park.

Josie laughed and said "That's why!"

They all watched as the irate golfer was cursing the driver of the Audi.

"He used to love watching from the window at the bar. Sometimes he would call me over to watch too. Ye wouldn't believe the number of times they would start fightin'. It was terrific." Josie looked back at the group and said "Yeah, that's definitely his favourite hole."

Graham looked at Melanie, who shrugged and said "Well at least my footwear is grateful. Even if I have to say I feel slightly embarrassed that we are going to scatter my husband's ashes in a puddle in a car park."

They walked over and gathered around the pothole which had taken on a different level of significance than before.

Melanie put the handbag down on the ground and fished out the urn, resting one hand on the lid.

"Would anyone like to say anything before I tip him into the hole?" Melanie asked, wincing at her own words.

"Yes please," Dorene said. "Stuart, I'll miss you. You're the best son anyone could have ever hoped for. Not as good as Graham of course," and she put her arm around Graham's arm, "but you did your best and you gave me the most wonderful grandson in the world." Dorene used her other arm and hooked it around Tom's on her other side, which meant she didn't have any hands free to wipe the tears that now trickled down her wrinkly cheeks.

"Can I say something?" Tom asked.

"Of course Tom," Graham said.

"Dad, I love you. I'm glad it was a heart attack that

killed you and I'm glad I haven't got the gene for it. I wish you had told me though. I'm going to come here and sit by the window and watch people getting soaked by your puddle and remember you forever." Tom looked up at Graham for reassurance that what he had said had been ok. Graham nodded approvingly.

Graham ended up saying a few clichés about how much he'd miss his brother but wished he had been able to come up with something more memorable. He looked at Melanie when he felt he had waffled on for long enough.

Melanie looked at Josie, Jack and Josh. They all shook their heads at the unspoken offer of saying something.

Melanie opened the lid and said "Stuart, I will miss you." She gently poured the content of the urn into the grey water of the pothole. They stood watching in silence as a few bubbles made it to the surface.

"Fancy a swally? Ah'm buying," Jack offered.

They all looked at each other, nodded, and walked to the clubhouse.

Tom ordered a pint of cider. Melanie and Dorene settled for white wine. Graham explained he had a taxi booked for three oclock for the airport and was worried about needing the loo if he had a pint.

"Ye bampot, 'cause ye need a pint," Jack said. "Where're ye gonnae go?" Jack wanted to know.

"To St Petersburg. It's a long story," Graham explained.

"He's meeting up with this giant gay porn star!" Tom announced and Graham could see other people at the bar turning their heads to get a look at who Tom was referring to.

"Well, it's not what you think," Graham said.

"No, of course not," Jack chuckled.

"He's my cousin and I found him on the internet," Graham explained.

"They look identical. You'd think they were twins!" Tom added.

"He is going to introduce me to his uncle Axel, who is my actual dad. Axel never married or had any children. He didn't know I existed until a week ago," Graham continued.

"That's pure dead brilliant! He isnae in the Russian mafia, is he?" Jack joked.

"He used to be the chairman of Gazprom. Not sure if that counts," Graham said and laughed.

"Jings! Ye'll inherit a fortune then? Ye know, St Petersburg is pretty rough, fancy taking me with ye as a bodyguard?"

Graham laughed and said firmly no.

He suddenly stopped and looked at Dorene and said "Is that what you said when we handed the money over to the kidnappers? Did you tell them my dad was the head of Gazprom?"

"No stupid, they would have asked for fifty million then, not fifty grand. What I said was… " and Dorene leant forward and whispered something into Graham's ear. Graham blushed and he wondered if he'd ever be able to look at his mum in the same way ever again.

*

Acknowledgements

You need something that drives you to spend hour after hour typing away at the keyboard. For me, it was Emma Kanis sending me emails like "Read, liked, want more!" or "Well I gobbled that up quickly, very tasty! Keep going, I look forward to the next instalment." Without someone eagerly waiting for what's going to happen next, it is far too easy to make excuses not to write. I would also like to thank Sam Johnson and Jane Beaumont for invaluable help with editing and proofreading and Richard Denny for not minding me going on and on about the book during our coffee breaks. Special thanks to Singletrackworld forum for being the font of all knowledge, in this case Glaswegian slang. Iain Cullen, Josh Alcock, Perchy Panther and seosamh77, thank you for your helpful suggestions.

About the Author

Emmy Hoyes was born in Sweden but now lives in the Yorkshire Dales with her dog Lily. "His Favourite Hole" is her first book and is a testament to the intriguing storylines you can come up with while dog-walking. When not daydreaming or writing, she is developing new software applications for analytical instrumentation or responding to mountain rescue call-outs.

To find out more about her books or sign up for her mailing list to not miss the next one please visit **https://emmyhoyes.com/books.html**

Graham's story hasn't finished yet...

Printed in Great Britain
by Amazon